The Pride

Kali Wardyn

Published by Kali Wardyn, 2022.

This is a work of fiction. Similarities to real people, places, or events are entirely coincidental.

THE PRIDE

First edition. May 11, 2022.

Copyright © 2022 Kali Wardyn.

ISBN: 979-8201996444

Written by Kali Wardyn.

Chapter 1

In the year 3564, a new planet was discovered. The scientist who discovered it named it Vulcan, after the Roman god of fire, as it was very hot on the planet. NASA had sent space probes and satellites to Vulcan, and had deemed it a planet that could be colonized. They were planning to send people there after they started developing buildings that could resist the almost unendurable heat. About ten years after the planet was discovered, buildings had been built, huge domes made of cement. NASA decided that was the year that people would be sent to Vulcan in an attempt to make a settlement there.

NASA sent out word about the new settlement, as volunteers were needed to fly to Vulcan and live there. The hot planet was very close to the sun, which made the journey extremely dangerous. There weren't many people that volunteered to go, but among the ones who did, was an adventurous young girl named Regan.

Regan was very excited to fly to Vulcan. She had asked her parents to volunteer after her best friend Rya's family offered to go. Rya could make anybody laugh, and she was popular wherever she went. Some of Regan's other friends, Emma and Katie, volunteered as well. The four friends hung out all the time, and couldn't imagine being apart.

There were families that had volunteered too, but they wouldn't be meeting them, as they would not be living together. The reason for this was that NASA was trying out different settlements all around the planet to see which areas worked best for life. The four girls had also been told that a transportation system was almost ready for use. It was the only reason they were allowed to go unsupervised, as they weren't going to be there very long without an adult.

There had also been a debate about just one family going at first and the rest following later. That had been shot down because, with kids, it'd be hard to figure out how to survive on the planet. They also couldn't send all the parents, because then the kids would have no mode of transportation and no one to care for them down on Earth. Although the teenagers were considered responsible enough to do it, they had little siblings too. So, they agreed on allowing the four girls to settle the planet alone for the first few days.

The flight was scheduled for September 14th. The four friends were to go to the Octagon, a large eight sided building, where they would receive their suits and equipment. They only needed the suits for the flight. Once they landed on the planet they were allowed to take them off. Most of the food provisions were already on the spaceship flying to Vulcan. Food had also already been stored on the planet, in the various buildings that had been built prior to their coming.

The night before takeoff, all who were going to Vulcan gathered their belongings and packed them in suitcases. Although the time apart would be temporary, the volunteers all clung to their loved ones as they said farewell. Family and friends leaned on the hope that the transportation system NASA was working on would be ready sooner rather than later.

The next day, the journey to Vulcan commenced. Regan was slightly nervous, but at the same time she was extremely excited. She would be one of the first people to live on a planet different from Earth!

After the long flight, the volunteers landed on Vulcan. The heat blasted their faces immediately. The planet's surface was made up of red rocks, lava pools, and fire-blasting volcanoes.

Regan found she had some small difficulty walking across the many red pebbles and chunks of glass as they walked toward the dome shaped buildings that were to be their homes. Each of them had at least two suitcases full of clothes, and their belongings were in totes in the back of the spaceship.

Regan walked up to the first dome in sight, a large gray mass of concrete. She passed through the entrance, a square cut in the dome, and although she was thankful for the air conditioning in the building, she was disappointed with what she saw. The big building had a small living room to the left of the front door. The couches and chairs were an ugly greenish brown color, the wood table was way too big for the tiny area, and the fuzzy yellow rug under the table smelled like rotten eggs. The kitchen beside it wasn't much better. The tile floors were broken and cracked, the fridge, which they'd been told was powered by the generator that also provided electricity for the air conditioner, both smelled and looked like moldy cheese, and the countertops were basically falling apart. The cabinets at least looked decent. The microwave didn't look terrible either.

Regan laid her suitcases beside the couch in the living room, as did the others, took off her space suit, and after retrieving the rest of their belongings from the space ship, went exploring. She found a small bathroom in the back of their new living quarters. It wasn't much better than what she'd already seen. She turned around to walk out of the bathroom when Emma came rushing up.

"We need help. Rya's fallen into a hole in her bedroom and she can't get out," she said quickly. She followed Emma through a wide hallway behind the bathroom into a big, spacious bedroom. It was meant for all of them to share, so the creators of the building had put small walls in between each bed so they had some privacy. A curtain hung in front of each bed, suspended from a curtain rod that connected to the two walls on either side of the mattress. Regan quickly found Rya holding herself up using only her arms. The hole she'd fallen in was several feet deep. It was a miracle that she hadn't fallen all the way through. Regan quickly jumped to one side of her, Emma on the other. They each grabbed an arm and hoisted her out of the hole.

"We'll need to fix that," Rya giggled as she looked down into the hole. If she wouldn't have caught herself, she could have easily broken a leg. Emma found a sheet of metal under her bed that was probably leftover from construction. Regan assumed the builders hadn't wanted to haul back to Earth. Carefully, they laid it over the hole.

"We'll just have to hope that stays. We need to find the medical equipment in case something like that happens again and someone gets injured," Regan stated. She wondered why the dome was in such disrepair since NASA had just built it. Rya had also voiced by then what a horrible designer NASA had hired, with the ugly colors of all the furniture.

The medical equipment was soon found by Katie in a cabinet in the kitchen. They explored a little more, but there wasn't much else to see. In addition to the giant bedroom and terrible bathroom, the hallway also provided entrance to an empty concrete room. The four volunteers moved each of their suitcases to their bedrooms. Then they all met in the kitchen for their first meal in their new home.

"There's nothing in the fridge, but I did find some chicken noodle soup cans in the pantry," said Katie, holding up three small cans of soup. One looked as if it had already been opened. The other two were dirty and covered in cobwebs.

"That can't possibly be all there is! NASA told us there would be food ready for us," exclaimed Emma. Regan agreed with a slow head nod.

Something strange was happening. First the house being wrecked, then there being virtually no food. She wondered what would be next.

They were in luck, however, as Rya, being always hungry, had snuck food on the spaceship. She had a bag of almonds, a small box of cheerios, and a bag of dried pineapple. Regan had also packed a bag of trail mix for Rya. The four girls rationed out the food the best they could. While they ate, they discussed what they had found while exploring the house.

"I found a snake in one of the kitchen cabinets," Katie told them. Regan shivered in disgust. She hated snakes, just like her mom did. She was surprised to find that she already missed her family and friends that were left behind.

"I think it's odd how this place seems so broken down after NASA told us they had just built the place," she told her friends. They nodded in agreement.

"What if there are aliens here? Maybe they're the ones that wrecked the place," mused Emma. She'd always been a little suspicious of the unknown.

"I don't know. Maybe we should take a trip outside in the morning and look around. We might find something then," said Regan. It seemed like a good idea.

"The sun won't rise and set the same as it did on Earth. How will we know when it is morning?" asked Katie. Regan reached into her pocket and pulled out a small, bronze pocket watch.

"This will tell us," she said. It was currently seven o'clock. Regan made a big deal about always being prepared for anything. Only on rare occasions could you find her unprepared.

"Well, it's settled then. Tomorrow we'll take a look outside and explore. Maybe we'll even find something edible while we're out. These snacks can't last us forever," Emma said. Indeed, the snacks were already a fourth of the way empty. Everyone was finished eating, and the four volunteers threw away the napkins they had been eating on and started getting ready for bed.

By the time everyone was ready to go to sleep, it was 8:30. Emma was yawning, and Katie was already asleep. Rya was boasting about how she would stay up all night, but her friends knew that if she did, she wouldn't wake up until lunch the next day. Rya liked her sleep. So, Regan made her go to bed by nine o'clock.

"Goodnight everyone," they said chorally, and then they fell asleep to dream of aliens and snakes.

Chapter 2

The next morning, Regan was the first one awake. She decided to go outside while the rest were sleeping. She wanted to be the first one to get a good look at their new environment. She dressed in black shorts and a red tank top. She tied back her dirty blonde hair, put on her shoes, and stepped outside. The heat blasted her, making her sweat. The first thing she saw was a huge volcano. It was in the act of erupting, and she thought it looked quite pretty in its sheer glory and power.

Then Regan saw a faint, worn down path winding toward what seemed to be a small cave. Her foot stopped mid step. If she went by herself and found something dangerous, she could be killed. Her friends would never know what had happened to her. Her adventurous spirit told her to go anyway and check it out. Maybe she could find something they could eat down in the cave. After a few steps and growing anticipation, her hesitant side won out, and she ran back to her new home to tell her friends what she had seen.

By the time she was back, everyone was awake and dressed. She walked into the kitchen where they had started handing out food rations.

"I'm so glad you're here!" exclaimed Rya, smiling in relief.

"We were so afraid you had been killed by aliens or something! Where were you?" asked Emma. Katie ran up and hugged her. Regan was a little taken aback. If she'd known they'd be this worried, she would have waited until everyone had gotten up.

"I went exploring outside. I figured the rest of you would be a while in waking up," she told them, "you know aliens aren't real, right?"

"Emma was the only one who was scared about aliens. The rest of us were worried you had run off and left us," said Rya. Her friends nodded. Regan couldn't believe it. How could her best friends think she would run off without them?

"I would never leave you guys," she told them. The four girls hugged.

"Alright, break it up," said Katie sarcastically. Regan chuckled.

"Yeah, let's eat," agreed Rya. The four friends sat down in the rotting wood chairs and ate their food on the rickety wood table. The table was barely big enough for all of them, and there was even less room to walk around the table. As Regan was eating, she remembered what she had seen outside.

"While I was outside, I found a path leading to a cave. I didn't follow it because I wanted to wait for you guys, but when we leave the house we should check it out," she told them.

"Sounds good to me," replied Emma.

"You know what sounds good to me? Eating more cheerios," announced Rya as she stuffed a spoonful of the honey flavored cereal into her mouth. Regan laughed.

As soon as they were done eating, the four friends headed outside. Regan led them to the path she had seen earlier. The faint trail was hard to see at times, so it was slow going following it. Eventually though, the four volunteers made it to the cave Regan had seen when she went outside the first time.

When the four girls stepped up to the mouth of the cave, they froze. It was very bright, and seemed extremely cold considering how hot Vulcan was. The cave, instead of being red like the surface of the planet, was a light blue color. There were many light colored crystals scattered around the floor of the cave, and crystal stalactites hung from the ceiling. The large crystal structures emitted a soft glow, illuminating the cave so that the girls could see. Regan went first, stepping through the mouth of the cave. Instantly she felt colder, and when she glanced back at her friends, she could see that they had started shivering.

"It's freezing in here!" shouted Rya as she gripped her arms across her chest to keep them from shaking. Her voice echoed down through the cave, and Regan thought she heard something moving.

"Did you guys hear that?" she asked. They nodded.

"What do you think it was?" asked Katie, her eyes wide. Regan shook her head and gave a shoulder shrug.

"I have no idea, but I'm about to find out," she replied. Carefully, she made her way down the gently sloping floor of the cave, her friends following slowly behind her.

After a few minutes of walking, the slope became level again. It went on for a few more feet, and then opened to a huge cavern. Regan couldn't quite see what was inside the cavern yet, so she advanced a little farther. She stopped when she was a few steps away from it, waiting for her friends to catch up. They had lagged a little behind, being scared of tripping on the crystals that covered the ground.

"Woah," whispered Emma in amazement as they entered the cavern. It was covered in white crystals that gave off an almost blinding light. Regan could faintly see the outline of what looked to be multiple large animals sleeping on the ground. After the initial shock of entering the cavern, their eyes began to adjust to the brilliant light. Regan began to make out the features of the animals. She thought she could see huge bat-like wings sticking out from the creatures' backs. They also looked like they had scales.

Suddenly, Rya took a step toward the creatures, accidentally kicking a rock and sending it racing toward one of the enormous animals' faces. Regan sucked in a breath, and her eyes went wide in terror at what might happen if that rock struck one of the animals. At the same time, however, she was curious about them. She wanted to know what the beasts were.

She was about to find out.

The rock had slowed down, and just barely bumped one of the large creatures. The great beast opened her eyes and slowly, she stood. She was well above ten feet tall, and was longer than two school buses. The giant animal had forest green scales all over her body and gigantic wings. Regan also noticed that the beast had huge claws at the end of her long legs. She opened her mouth to yawn, and Regan could see her big fangs.

"A-a dragon," she gasped in wonder. She had thought they were fake. Never in her life had she ever imagined she would ever see a dragon in real life. Her friends were equally amazed as the dragon stretched its mighty wings, drawing itself up to its full size.

Three other dragons lay next to where the green dragon stood. The white dragon was much smaller than the green one. She had a pointed spike on the end of her tail, whereas the green dragon had something that sort of resembled the head of a mace. There was a third dragon that had red scales and was smaller than the green dragon, yet still bigger than the white one. He had many spikes atop his head, making it look like he wore a crown of them. The largest of the four dragons was the black dragon. He had a big pair of horns angled back toward his tail. The tips of his wings ended in large spikes, and his tail ended in a spike that looked like a triangle, like the white dragon's tail.

By now all of the dragons had woken up; their big, golden eyes shone fiercely in the bright light of the cave.

As the four girls stood watching them, the dragons started lumbering toward them. This frightened Katie, who was extremely nervous around anything new, not to mention big, scary dragons. Katie ran out of the cave, making a lot of noise as she went. The noises alerted the dragons, who immediately began sniffing the air for traces of who caused the noise.

"Uh, we'd better be going now," stammered Emma. She too ran out of the cave. Only Rya and Regan were left.

Emma's voice had given away the two best friends' location. The dragons glared at the two girls. Regan felt small, which, compared to them, she was. The black dragon stalked toward them. Regan and Rya backed up as fast as they could without infuriating the dragons.

Only Rya made it out of the dragons' reach in time. Regan had gotten her foot caught on one of the various crystals littering the floor. She couldn't get it unstuck without angering the dragons. She tried to dislodge it carefully, but it wouldn't work.

When she looked up from what she was doing, she saw that the black dragon had gotten much closer than he'd originally been. Regan closed her eyes and braced herself, waiting for the dragon to devour her.

All Regan felt, however, was the dragon's hot breath on her face as he sniffed her. Slowly, she opened her eyes. The dragon's huge face was right in front of her. He seemed to be waiting for her to do something.

Rya must've read Regan's intentions on her face because as soon as Regan started raising her hand she whispered forcefully, "Whatever it is you're planning to do, don't do it!"

But Regan ignored her. She kept raising her hand as slowly as she could, so she wouldn't scare the dragon. The dragon leaned his head forward, and she placed her hand on his nose, and petted the beast. He started making a sound that sounded like a cat's purr, although it was about twenty times louder. Regan brought up her other hand and started scratching the dragon under his chin. The purring noise got louder.

"Amazing," she breathed in wonder at the magnificent beast before her. Rya looked equally astonished. Gradually, Regan pulled her hands away. The black dragon nudged her, asking for more.

"Not right now, big guy," she told him. She smiled. After a few seconds of struggling, she freed her foot, and began climbing back up to Rya. The dragon started to whine.

"I'll be back, don't worry," she murmured softly. Rya was staring at her slack jawed.

"How did you do that?" she asked incredulously. Regan shrugged.

"I have no idea," They hurried back home, where they found Emma and Katie making dinner with shaking hands. Regan instantly felt guilty. She knew they'd been scared. She should've hurried back to ease their fear.

As they burst in through the door, Emma and Katie rushed to meet them.

"We were so scared for you!" Katie said in a shaking voice. Regan hugged her. Katie was a person who could get scared very easily.

"Yeah," added Emma, "we thought the dragons might eat you alive! How did you guys escape?"

Rya answered, "The dragons didn't even try to eat us. The huge black one was right up in Regan's face, and he let her pet him!" Emma and Katie gaped at Regan in shock.

"H-How?" stuttered Katie.

Regan shrugged. "I have absolutely no idea. He came up and started sniffing me, so I tried touching him. I think he liked it. He started making a purring noise."

"Like a cat," Rya added knowingly. Rya had about twenty cats at her parents' farm on Earth. She was definitely a cat person.

"Wait a minute. Since the black dragon let Regan pet it, do you think that somehow, we could tame them?" suggested Emma. Regan had actually been wondering the same thing.

"Maybe," she answered doubtfully with a shrug and a downcast gaze. Although she desperately wanted to believe that they could tame them, she didn't want to get her hopes up. Dragons were the wildest animals, according to the myths and legends. There wasn't any guarantee they would be able to do it, if they were even brave enough to try.

"I call the green one!" shouted Rya. Regan smiled slightly. You could always count on Rya to rush into things without any sort of plan.

"It's not that simple, Rya," Regan said as she ran into her room to get a notepad. Her friends glanced at each other, confusion written on their faces. Regan came back with a small pad of paper and a yellow pencil in her hand. She sat on the greenish brown chair, her friends across from her on the couch. Regan flipped to the first clean page and wrote down *dragon taming* at the top of the sheet.

"What's the paper for?" asked Katie.

"Well, seeing as none of us have ever tamed a dragon before, I thought it would be a good idea to write down some ideas before we decide on what to do," she told them with only a hint of exasperation in her voice.

"Ooh, I have an idea!" gushed Rya, raising her hand as she had done when she was in elementary school.

"Yes, Rya?" answered Regan in her best teacher voice. Emma and Katie noticed what she was doing, and began giggling quietly. Yet Rya was oblivious to what was going on because she was so excited.

"We should get some steaks or some type of meat and feed them! Then they'll trust us!" she exclaimed.

"Might I ask a question, Rya?" Regan asked, still using her teacher voice. This only served to make Emma and Katie giggle harder. Rya, however, still did not notice.

"Exactly how are we supposed to get these steaks?" Katie and Emma died laughing. Rya was stumped for a moment, her brows furrowed in concentration as she tried to think of a way to get something a dragon would find appetizing.

Finally, she gave up. "I don't know." Then Emma's eyes lit up.

"What if there is a way to get meat on this planet? If there are dragons here, there has to be something for them to eat. We just have to find it!" The more Regan thought about it, the more it made sense. No animal could live without food or water, so there had to be something on Vulcan that the dragons ate, whether it be plants or other living creatures. She doubted they were herbivores because of their sharp teeth. Besides, all the plants she had seen so far looked either poisonous or dead.

"True, we should go exploring and see if we can find anything," she suggested to her friends.

"Tomorrow?" asked Katie. She was still a little shaken from seeing the dragons.

"Yes tomorrow! Who doesn't want a pet dragon?" Rya asked excitedly. She jumped up and ran to the bedrooms. She came back out with a pair of binoculars.

"Alright, all set!" she announced with a smile.

"Okay, two questions. One, why did you bring binoculars here? Two, why do we need those?" asked Regan. Rya gaped at her.

"These are my grandma's binoculars!" she said dramatically. "They go with me everywhere, and we need them because if we use them we won't have to walk as far to see things up close."

"Trust Rya to take the lazy way," teased Regan.

"You know me so well!" Rya laughed.

Chapter 3

The next morning, after finishing off the last bit of food, the four best friends went outside and searched for anything edible. They each had a small wicker basket with them to hold anything they found.

While Regan was looking, she came upon an animal that looked like a brown raccoon with a short, stubby tail. She ignored it because she had nothing to kill it with, and she couldn't put it in her basket. It was too large. Yet, when she tried to walk away from it, the short furred animal started following her.

She kicked at the animal, and it ran away. As soon as she turned her back, however, it came back.

She kicked at it again. "Go away!" Still the animal followed her. Finally, she set down her basket and rushed at the small animal, waving her hands around. This time it stayed away for good.

After a few more hours of searching, she found a grove of berry bushes. These were the first edible looking plants she had seen throughout her time on Vulcan. The berries were dark pink. They were also small and round. She picked a few, but made a mental note not to eat them until she was sure they weren't poisonous.

When it was time to meet up with her friends again, she had the pink berries and another fruit that looked like a light orange coconut, with a hard, fuzzy outer shell. She had cracked one of the fruits open when she had found it and saw that the inside was bright white. She knew it wasn't toxic because she had seen another one of the raccoon animals eating one.

Her friends had been successful as well. Katie had found some of the pink berries and a root vegetable that resembled a potato. Emma had found some herbs she wanted to try to use to make healing poultices and use for spices.

Then there was Rya.

"You won't believe what I found!" she announced hurriedly as she opened the lid of her wicker basket to reveal a small, tan, scaled animal. It had bright yellow eyes, floppy ears, and a long tail that curled around the animal's four webbed feet. There were spikes running along its back all the way to its tail.

"What is that?" exclaimed Katie. She backed away from it, holding her hands to her mouth and chewing her nails. Rya smiled proudly, grabbed it out of the basket, and held it up for everyone to see.

"This, my friends, is what I call a Ryzard! It's named after me. They're harmless!" Regan shook her head and laughed. Katie warmed a bit to the scaly creature now that she knew it wouldn't hurt her.

"Will the dragons eat something that small?" asked Emma thoughtfully. Rya shrugged.

"Only one way to find out." She placed the animal back in the basket. In addition to the lizard, she had found a substance that tasted sweet like sugar, and seedless berries that were purple and square shaped. Emma suggested they call the purple berries heliotropes, after a purple flower back on Earth.

When the four friends got back to the dome, it was starting to get dark. Night came about five hours later than on Earth, which had messed up their sleeping schedule for a while until they got used to the new time zone. Emma, the best chef of the four volunteers, decided she would make a fruit salad for dinner using what they had found. She mixed the pink berries and the heliotropes with the sugar Rya had found and took large slices of the coconut and chopped them up into cubes. What was leftover she put in the fridge.

When they sat down to eat, Rya's chair broke because one of the legs had a crack in it and snapped off. She had been sitting on her knees, and when she fell on them, she immediately started whining about them hurting.

Regan pulled up a footstool from the living room, "Here, use this." Rya looked at her gratefully as Regan held her hand out to help her up. Rya sank onto the footstool with a sigh.

"This is much more comfortable than that old thing," she said, nodding toward the chair. Regan smiled.

"So, how is it?" asked Emma after they'd started eating. Regan held up a thumb.

"Really good," answered Katie, interpreting Regan's gesture for Emma. Rya nodded in agreement.

"You're an amazing chef," Rya remarked, stuffing food into her mouth. Katie glared at her.

"Table manners, Rya?"

"Sorry," she said apologetically. She started eating slower and more carefully.

When they were done they washed the dishes and got ready for bed. As she climbed under the blankets, Regan thought about her home back on Earth. She missed the big yard and the red barn where her family hung out. She missed her room with her big blue bed. But most of all, she missed her parents, Holly and Paul, and her two sisters, Liza and Audrey. After about half an hour, she finally fell asleep. Her dreams were full of family and friends back on her old planet.

Chapter 4

The next morning, the four friends headed back to the dragons' cave. They brought Rya's lizard with them. Katie almost didn't go, but decided to follow and stay far behind with Emma and watch while Rya and Regan gave the lizard to the dragons.

The walk to the cave was full of hopeful discussion about the dragons.

"Just so you all know, the green dragon is mine," stated Rya. Regan smirked, they weren't even sure if the dragons could be tamed. Even though she hadn't wanted to get her hopes up about the mystical creatures, Regan knew that she wanted the black dragon.

"That's fine with me. I think the red one is the coolest," said Emma.

"You can have the black one, Regan. I'd rather own the nice, little white dragon," said Katie fearfully. They all knew Katie was terrified of the dragons, so it was a miracle she even wanted one at all.

"Okay," she replied. Secretly though, Regan was overjoyed. She knew she could tame the dragons with the help of her friends.

After a few minutes of walking, they came to the cave. Regan went first because the dragons were familiar with her. Rya carried the lizard, and Emma and Katie followed behind. When they neared the cavern where they had seen the dragons sleeping, the four girls could see the animals flying high up near the ceiling.

Pretty soon, however, the dragons spotted them. The black dragon dropped down near the entrance to the cavern and walked the rest of the way toward them. As he came near, Regan lifted up her hand for him to sniff. Once he recognized who it was, he shoved his head into her hand so she could pet him. The force of it knocked her over into Rya. Rya almost dropped the lizard they'd brought, but managed to hold onto it by the tail. The black dragon offered Regan his head to help her stand up. After she was on her feet, she held out a hand to Rya.

"You can give the lizard to him," said Regan. Rya shook her head.

"I want to give it to my dragon." Regan turned to the black dragon. His golden eyes shone in the crystal light.

"I know you probably don't understand me, but can you bring your friend over here?" she asked him, pointing her head toward the green dragon, which was just landing for a nap. He must have understood though, because as soon as she was done talking, he growled at the female dragon. She flew over gracefully, landing with barely any noise, which was a considerable achievement given her size. Rya offered the lizard to her, which she sniffed and ate in a couple of bites.

"I think she liked it," Rya noted as the dragon began sniffing her all over. As she was watching, Regan noticed the red and white dragon start to come over to the group. She waved over Emma and Katie, who slowly tip toed over. Katie was shaking uncontrollably, but Emma seemed calm. When they came up to their dragons, each was sniffed and then purred at as they pet them. Katie started to calm down when her dragon laid down at her feet. Katie sat down next to her, and stroked the dragon's pearly white scales.

After about an hour of getting acquainted with their new friends, the four girls left. When all the dragons began whining and trying to follow them, they shushed them and told them they'd be back tomorrow. Eventually, they made it out of the cave. Regan could still hear the dragons' whining behind her.

"I'd say that went well," she said happily. Emma nodded in agreement. Katie seemed to have thought so too.

"Yeah, did you see me? I was petting her, actually petting her!" she exclaimed. Regan was proud of her. She definitely wasn't as afraid of them now.

"You did awesome!" replied Rya, patting Katie on the back. Katie, being small, was pushed forward a little by the impact.

She rubbed her hit shoulder. "Yeah, I guess I did."

As they walked back home, Regan thought about the black dragon. Then, she realized the dragons needed names. This she voiced to her friends, who agreed eagerly.

"I'm naming mine Angel," said Katie. Her dragon was surely an angel. She was the nicest of the four beasts. Emma stroked her chin, but then her face lit up.

"Mine's Ember," she said triumphantly. Rya looked extremely excited.

"Wait till you hear my name! Drumroll, please," she hit her legs to make it sound like a drum, "Yoda!" Regan sighed at her friend's ignorance.

"Rya, the green dragon is a girl," she told her. Rya slumped.

"What about Terra? From *Teen Titans*?" suggested Emma, a name from a TV show they used to watch as kids.

"Too childish," Rya said.

"And Yoda isn't?" Emma shot back good-naturedly.

"Nakata? I'm pretty sure there is a famous dragon named that," offered Regan. Rya's face lit up.

"Well, my dragon's going to be famous. Nakata it is!" she exclaimed, happy to have found a name she liked. That left Regan.

"What are you naming your dragon?" asked Katie. The more Regan thought about the black dragon, the more she wanted it. Yet, she had no idea what a good name would be.

Then, she heard a loud roar and the beating of wings. She looked up and saw the black dragon flying toward them. The three other dragons weren't far behind. She could just barely see the dragon's dark scales glimmering against the dark sky.

"Nyx," she said as the dragon landed next to her with a thud. "It means night. I'm pretty sure there was something about it in that one Greek mythology class we took last year."

The dragons followed them the rest of the way home. The next morning, the girls found them asleep inside one of the other domes. The dome had its top ripped off before the volunteers came to Vulcan, most likely by an especially strong wind storm, and the dragons had flown in through the hole and gone to bed.

"We should make that their new nest," suggested Katie. The four beasts didn't look very comfortable. Once the dragons woke up, they started working on making the nest more homelike for their new friends. The girls gathered giant sticks from the trees outside and mattresses from inside the other domes. They cleared all the furniture out from the nest and threw it in an extra dome. Then they dragged in the mattresses and sticks and scattered them around the nest for bedding. The inner walls had been crushed when the dragons' flew in the night before, adding chunks of concrete to the list of things they'd had to remove from the building. After they were done, the place looked more like a bird's nest than a house for humans. The dragons loved it. The second the girls left, they curled up in the soft bedding and took a long nap.

"Looks good," stated Regan as she shook her hands free of dust that had settled on the mattresses. Her friends agreed. If this was going to be the dragons' new home they should feel comfy and secure. The volunteers had decided not to fix the roof because they doubted anything would be able to swoop in and kill the dragons in their sleep, considering the fact that their scales provided a thick armor. Plus they made for an intimidating animal, with their large horns, giant claws, and sharp teeth.

Fixing up the nest had taken the majority of the day. Regan and her friends had skipped lunch in favor of finishing the dome before dark. All of them were starving, Katie most of all. She had put in the most work, saying the massive animals deserved a nice home.

Emma cooked again, with the help of Regan. Rya and Katie were cleaning up the girls' own home, dusting and sweeping with makeshift brooms they had made using the broken pieces of the sticks.

"I wish we had some meat to use. Without protein, it's going to be really hard to keep our strength up," said Emma. It was true. Tonight would be the only night since they'd come to Vulcan on which they would eat true meat because Rya had found some more chicken noodle soup cans while they'd been looking for bedding.

"What if we asked the dragons to hunt for us?" she asked. Emma glanced at her in the midst of her stirring the thick soup.

"You really think that'd work? How do we know they can understand us when we talk?" Emma gave Regan the pot with the soup, which Regan then put on the small oven they'd been supplied with. The oven could barely fit the medium sized pot on it, as it was so small. She turned the black knob above the oven door to high, heating up the soup.

"Well, Nyx must've understood when I asked him to call Nakata over in the cave," she replied. Emma still looked doubtful.

"Well, I guess it's worth a shot," she amended. They finished the soup just as Rya and Katie walked in. Both were covered in feathers and smelled atrocious.

"We went outside to shake out the rug in the living room and were attacked by some dog-like thing! He had eight legs though, and four eyes. He knocked me and Katie into the dragons' kill pile! It was seriously gross in there, with all the rotting animals and stuff!" explained Rya in a shaky voice through a mouthful of feathers. It sounded quite funny.

"Don't worry though, Angel took care of the dog," said Katie. Regan tried hard not to laugh, and she could see that Emma was turning red from holding her breath, not wanting to embarrass her friends by laughing at them.

"You should go get cleaned up before you eat," Regan managed to choke out. Rya and Katie trudged toward the bathroom. As soon as they were gone, Regan burst out laughing, and Emma joined her. By the time they were done, both had tears in their eyes. Never in her life had Regan seen something as funny as her two friends covered in bird feathers and dust.

Regan composed herself quickly though as Katie and Rya came back to help set the table. Emma was not as successful hiding her emotions, but gladly, their friends didn't notice.

Over the flavorless soup, Emma told Rya and Katie about Regan's idea to ask the dragons to hunt for them. Rya was optimistic about it, as she was about everything. Katie, surprisingly, was all for it.

"I think it'll work. It'd be one less thing for us to worry about, and it gives the dragons something to do in their free time," she said.

"Yeah, exactly. One thing about this soup though, Emma, if I'm being honest, it's awful," said Rya as she spooned a mouthful of the cloudy broth into her mouth. She almost choked as she swallowed it, forcing it down with a glass of water. The fridge's water dispenser didn't work, but when they had first come to the house they'd seen a stream of water next to the dome, weaving through the many homes scattered around the area. Next to the door had been a wooden bucket, which they used to scoop up the water. It was where they got the water to shower, drink, and wash their clothes.

"It's because it's from a can. Canned soups are always terrible. But, it was the only thing left to eat," she explained sadly. Emma was a proud chef, and when someone said her food was bad it hurt her feelings.

"I don't blame you for it. That's not something you can control," consoled Regan as she glared pointedly at Rya. She shrank back in her seat.

"Yeah, not much you can do about that," Rya mumbled. Emma was happier after that, though still not as cheerful as she'd been before they started the meal.

They finished the meal, and went to bed early so they would be rested for the morning. They had a busy day planned. They were going to, of course, ask the dragons about hunting, and then they wanted to forage for more food. They hoped to stock up on fruits and vegetables. They would have to see about meat, depending on what the dragons did about hunting for them.

When she woke up, Regan went to go ask Nyx to hunt. They had absolutely no food in the house, so breakfast wasn't an option. She ran to the dragons' nest, where Nyx was just getting up. She watched as he stretched his long, powerful legs in the rising sun, his scales glittering like stars. Shortly after he finished stretching, he spotted her standing in the doorway. The black beast bounded over in long strides and shoved his face into her hand, the force of which almost knocked her to the ground. Laughing, she stroked his neck and he started purring.

"Nyx," she said, "I need to ask you a favor. Is there any chance that you and your friends could help us hunt for food?" Nyx stepped back and turned so that his left side was facing her. He let one of his wings touch the ground and gestured with his head toward his back.

"You want me to get on your back?" Regan asked incredulously. The dragon nodded. Carefully, Regan climbed up his wing and sat on his back. She leaned forward slowly and threw her arms around his neck. The dragon lifted up his wings and took off.

"Woah!" yelled Regan as she soared over the rocky surface of Vulcan. She could hear Nyx's wings beating as he flapped them. She spread out her arms, holding on only with her legs. She felt the wind flowing through her hair. Her eyes watered from the speed. It was exhilarating.

"This is awesome!" Suddenly, Nyx veered off to the left, and then Regan spotted a large animal drinking water from a small stream. She put her arms back around his neck as he dove for the animal. She had to scrunch her eyes to keep them from watering.

When he came back up from the dive, Nyx had a large mammal hanging from his claws. It was like a bison, but its fur was short and it had enormous horns that curled back toward its long tail. The animal was still alive, and it struggled to get out of the dragon's tight grip. Soon, however, it gave up, and hung limply until they got back to the house. Then, Nyx dropped it while they were still very high up. The animal landed with a loud thud, causing her friends, who had woken up almost right after Regan had left, to come running out of the house. Regan waved to them as they stared slack jawed at her and Nyx.

"C'mon! You gotta try this! It's awesome!" she yelled down to them as Nyx swooped down, landing next to them with another thud. Regan slid to the ground and would've fallen if Rya hadn't caught her.

"How in the world did you manage to get him to let you ride him?" Katie asked, still in shock.

"It was Nyx's idea. He told me to get on his back," Regan answered.

"He told you? Regan, he's a dragon, he can't speak," said Emma. Regan turned to pet Nyx's neck.

"I'd like to disagree. When I told him about hunting, he let me climb on his back. He nodded when I asked if that was what he wanted," Regan told them.

"Well, what are we waiting for?" exclaimed Rya as she rushed after Nyx, who had left to go back to the nest. Regan, Katie, and Emma ran after her. By the time they got to the nest, all of them were out of breath.

"Rya, next time you rush off, you're doing it by yourself," panted Emma as she tried to slow down her breathing.

"Well, you didn't have to follow me," said Rya as she walked through the entrance to the nest. Regan raised an eyebrow.

"Uh huh, sure." They followed her in to see the dragons all lined up, waiting for the girls to get on their backs.

"Um, wh-what if w-we fall?" stammered Katie. Regan knew she was terrified.

"I don't think you will, but just in case, we can rig up a safety saddle for you if that's what you want," Regan said to her. Katie's shaking ceased.

"Okay, that sounds good." Regan took some of the sticks and placed them in a square shape. She stuck them together with some adhesive she had brought with her on the spaceship. When she held the contraption up for everyone to see, it looked like a box of sticks. Yet, there was no bottom so Katie could still sit on Angel's back, and there were bars on the top, wide enough apart that Katie could still stick her upper body out, but close enough that Katie wouldn't fall out. Regan took a long piece of leather, which she had ripped from a couch in one of the other domes, and stuck it to one side of the box. The other side she used Velcro strips to attach it to the box.

"Where did you get the Velcro?" asked Emma curiously.

"I brought it with me from my work shed at home. You never know what you might need on a strange planet," she answered as she finished strapping the makeshift safety device to Angel's back. Angel didn't seem to mind it that much. Regan figured that the white dragon knew about Katie being scared. The dragons seemed pretty smart.

"Why didn't you just glue the thing around Angel's back in the first place?" asked Rya. Katie glanced at her.

"Yeah, I suppose it would be nice to sleep with a box on your back," she said sarcastically, "It's so you can take it off."

"Oh, that makes sense," Rya acknowledged. After Regan finished rigging up the safety box, her three friends mounted the dragons. Regan had decided earlier that she was going to give Nyx a break.

"Woah, easy there fella," said Emma as her dragon shifted his feet. Ember was just as nervous as Emma was, Regan realized. She shouted this to her friend, who then tried to calm him down with soothing words. It seemed to work, as the dragon stopped moving and his breath came slower.

"Alright, have fun!" shouted Regan as her friends took off. She could hear them screaming with joy as she walked back to the house. Nyx had fallen asleep; he had woken up pretty early for a dragon. Normally the dragons slept till noon.

When Regan walked into the house, she went to her bedroom and opened her black backpack. She grabbed the book she had brought and opened it. It was her favorite book, *Call of the Wild*. She loved the way the author, Jack London, made it sound like a poem, yet it was still a story.

She was still reading by the time her friends got back from their ride. She rushed to greet them at the door.

"Regan! You won't believe what we found!" exclaimed Katie. Her friends' cheeks were red from the wind and heat, but all of them were smiling with joy.

"What?" she prompted. Rya was jumping up and down in her excitement.

"We found people!" they shouted in unison. Regan gaped at them.

"Where?"

"While we were flying, we spotted a tunnel. We were watching when we saw humans come out! It's only a couple of miles away!" said Emma.

"Did they look like humans?"

"Yeah, except they were really red. We thought it was sunburn," said Katie. Regan still found it hard to believe.

"But NASA told us we were the first to settle here?"

"Yeah, they also told us there would be food here," stated Rya sarcastically.

"True," amended Regan, "Did they see you?"

"No we were too high up," answered Emma.

"We can take you there tomorrow!" Katie told her. It was already getting dark.

"Okay. We should see if these 'humans' know English," said Regan.

"Yeah, but for now, let's make supper. I'm starving!" said Rya. Emma shook her head.

"We don't have anything to cook."

"Hey, what about the big bison thingy Nyx killed this morning?" suggested Regan.

"Might work, but Rya has to cook this time," said Emma.

"Fine," she grumbled as she went out to cut some meat from the bison.

Rya, it turned out, was a good chef. She had cooked the bison so it was tender and juicy, and each of the girls ate their fill. It was the first decent meal they'd had while living on Vulcan. They cleaned their plates pretty quickly.

"Should we feed the dragons?" asked Katie as she finished up washing her plate. They looked out the window next to the front door.

"I'd say they're fine," said Emma. The dragons were tearing through the kill pile, feathers and fur flying everywhere.

"And you say I'm a messy eater," laughed Rya. Regan wondered if this was how they always ate.

When they were done cleaning up the table, they got ready for bed. When Regan slid into bed, she began thinking about the people her friends said they had seen. What could this mean for us and the people back at Earth, she asked herself. She knew nothing about these strange humans, but she knew in her heart something was wrong about them coming here. First the houses being demolished, then there being no food.

"I'll figure it out in the morning." She closed her eyes and slept, thinking about red-faced people destroying her home planet.

When she woke up, she got dressed and headed for the kitchen. Katie and Emma were already up.

"Look! I made breakfast!" shouted Katie excitedly.

"Shhh, Rya is still sleeping. You know she needs her beauty rest," Regan teased.

"Sorry," whispered Katie. She was still smiling, however, as she held up a plate of what looked like sausages.

"Did those come from the bison?" Regan had butchered pigs before at her grandpa's farm when she was little. She knew sausage came from hogs, and bison were definitely not pigs.

"No, I saw Ember go hunting this morning. He brought a pig back. Who knew they had pigs on this planet?" said Emma.

"So the hunting plan worked then?" Regan took a bite of the sausage looking meat. It tasted just like the sausage back home, salty and greasy. She wondered how, since sausage, like bacon, had a process for being cured before it could be eaten.

"I guess so. What else would explain how Ember dropped it on the doorstep?" Emma also seemed to like the sausage-type meat. Regan had seen her eat at least two already, and the patties were the size of Emma's hand.

"Must've been a big piggy." Katie nodded.

"Yeah, you should've seen it! It was as big as the bison yesterday!" she exclaimed.

"Which was nine feet long. I measured it," said Emma, pulling out a measuring tape from the back pocket of her jeans.

"Measured what?' asked Rya sleepily as she trudged into the kitchen.

"Look, sleeping beauty is up!" laughed Regan. Rya rubbed her eyes.

"I'm not sleeping beauty," she yawned. She took a deep breath and smelled the sausage cooking on the stove. Instantly her eyes lit up.

"What's that?" Emma and Katie told her the story of Ember and the nine foot long pig. When they were finished, Rya grabbed a patty and took a huge bite.

"This is really good," she mumbled through a mouthful of food.

"Manners, Rya," Katie reminded.

"Sorry."

Regan laughed. "She's never going to learn," she told Katie.

"Probably not," she admitted.

"So, when do you guys want to show me these 'people' you found?" Regan was very curious about the people. She wanted to learn more about them, see if they were real humans or just strange animals that looked like people.

"Well, we should do it after we finish eating. It might take us a while to find them again," Emma answered.

"Wait, you don't remember where they were?" Regan asked incredulously. She found it hard to believe that someone could be so excited about something and then forget where the thing was.

"Well, not exactly," Rya said.

"Do you think the dragons remember where it was?" asked Katie.

"I don't know. It's worth a shot though," Regan answered. As soon as they were done with breakfast, the four girls headed out to the nest.

"I've never realized how big these things are," stated Katie as they approached the huge dome. It towered over them, casting a long shadow over their faces.

"Yeah, now that I think about it, all of them are at least as tall as the water tower back home," said Regan, thinking about her old town. She passed over the threshold of the doorway, entering the nest to find the four dragons sleeping.

"Well, now what?" asked Katie. Just as she finished speaking, Nyx and Nakata opened their eyes. Nakata stood up and stretched, and in the process of doing so, bumped Ember's flank. The red dragon snarled at her, and the loud noise woke up Angel.

"Solved that problem," laughed Regan. Nyx seemed to sense her intention of riding him, as he again invited her onto his back.

"Look how smart they are!" exclaimed Katie as Angel nudged the contraption Regan had made the day before for Katie's safety.

"Don't you want to ride without it?" asked Emma. Katie shook her head.

"No, no way. Way too scary," she answered. Regan smiled.

"I don't care what you guys say, Nakata is the best dragon!" declared Rya as she mounted the big female.

"No way! Ember's the best!" shouted Emma. She was already seated on the red beast. His crown of spikes looked menacing in the vicious sunlight.

"Angel is better! She's so nice!" argued Katie. She must have been practicing, because now she could strap on her box-like device without any help. Regan climbed onto Nyx's back with ease.

"We both know that you are the best dragon out there," she whispered to him. He snorted in agreement.

"Uh, can I get a little help?" asked Katie. She was having trouble mounting Angel because of how tiny she was. Katie was a short and skinny person, and didn't yet have the strength to pull herself all the way up. Angel didn't make a ramp with her wing like Nyx did because her wings were so small and dainty. If you wanted to ride Angel, you had to pull yourself up.

"Yeah, I'm coming," Regan said as she dismounted Nyx. She ran over and pushed Katie up to Angel's back, where Katie then climbed into the safety box.

"All set! Thanks, Regan!"

"No problem!" she shouted over her shoulder as she ran up Nyx's wing to his back. The black dragon's wings were two inches thick, and strong enough to carry his enormous body.

"Everyone ready?" Regan asked loudly.

"Yep!" her friends answered in unison. All four dragons took off with a low whoosh. The animals rose rapidly, their wings sounding like drums as they beat the air.

"Alright, Nakata! Show us the way to the people we saw yesterday," commanded Rya. The green dragon huffed in answer, and veered sharply right. She took them past a small lava lake. The magma was bubbling and spewing smoke.

"You recognize that lava?" asked Regan. Emma nodded.

"Yeah, the smoke was a lot worse yesterday!" she shouted over the beating of wings.

We'll have to work on being quieter if we don't want the people to notice us, thought Regan. It would be quite a job, but she was sure they could do it with lots of practice.

"Hey, I think I see it!" Rya shouted, interrupting Regan's thoughts. Sure enough, Regan could see what looked like people roaming around the entrance to a tunnel.

"Let's land near them," said Emma. The dragons swooped down and landed with a thud several yards away from the dark mouth of the tunnel. The people stared at them as they dismounted their dragons, pausing what they were doing to gape at them. They had probably never seen someone that wasn't someone they knew, Regan realized.

"Alright, let's not seem too overbearing," Regan whispered to her friends as they approached the red-faced humans. They saw one of them run over and ring a bell, making a loud ringing noise. This caused everyone to go scrambling into the tunnel.

"Well, that went well," laughed Regan. Then the girls saw two people going against the crowd, walking toward them. One was a girl with long, red hair and startling green eyes. The other, a boy, had red dreadlocks falling around his face. The boy, however, had brown eyes, similar to Regan's own, which she had always thought were a very odd color. It wasn't hazel, but it wasn't a dark brown either. Both of them looked to be about Regan's age, were small, and had wiry muscles, like they worked constantly.

"Hello, my name is Ann," said the girl warily. Her voice was gruff, her accent making the words difficult to understand, yet not impossible.

"Hi, Ann. I'm Rya!" Rya, being ever impulsive, had done the exact opposite of what Regan had said earlier.

"This is Katie, Emma, and I'm Regan," said Regan pointing to her friends. She glared at Rya, but her best friend shook it off.

"Hello girls, my name is Brian," said the boy, his red hair shining in the sun. "Ann is my sister, and we are the leaders of the Pride. What brings you here?"

"Well, my friends here were flying around yesterday and spotted some of you walking about," explained Regan.

"Yeah! We wanted to see if you knew anything about Earth!" said Rya hurriedly. Again, Regan glared at her. She was giving away too much information before they knew if this, 'Pride,' was friendly or not.

"What is Earth?" asked Brian.

"It's our home planet! You see, we weren't born here, we flew here on a spaceship! Now we live here!" said Rya in an excited voice. Ann looked thoughtful for a minute.

"Could you tell us more about this, Earth?" she asked. Rya started to answer, but was interrupted by Regan.

"Enough about us, what about you? Were you born here?" asked Regan.

"In fact, yes. Ann and I are twins. We inherited leadership over the Pride when our mother, Wendy, passed away a few years ago," Brian answered sadly. He lowered his head to look at the ground.

"Oh, I'm sorry," said Emma with a downcast gaze.

"What's the Pride?" Rya asked. Ann nodded for Brian to answer.

"Well, the Pride is the group of people that live here. Of course, there are a few people living on this planet who aren't included in the association, but everyone on the planet who didn't come from your Earth was born in the Pride."

"Why aren't they with you anymore?" asked Katie. The dragons were getting bored and had started playing with each other, flapping their wings and fighting. One certain gust of wind, caused by Nyx's enormous wings, blew a storm of dust into the six talking people, who coughed when it hit them.

"They broke a set of rules the first leaders of the Pride established in its early days. The punishment for breaking those rules is banishment from the Pride and its home," Brian choked out through the dust.

"What are those things?" asked Ann, pointing at the dragons.

"Dragons," Regan answered.

"No, dragons cannot be tamed like this. It must be some sort of offbreed. Have they ever done anything magical, like breathe fire? That is how you determine if it is a dragon," Ann stated.

"Well, no..." Rya trailed off. As soon as she had started talking Ember spewed a stream of fire. It charred the ground around him, making the rocky surface black. Smoke rose around him in tendrils, curling around his face and crown of spikes.

"I'd say that's a dragon then," smiled Emma.

"They get their powers around nine months of age and stop growing at twelve. They must be around nine months of age," said Ann.

"How did you manage to tame those things?" asked Brian in utter disbelief.

"Well, first of all, only Ember has shown he has powers. Second, they aren't very vicious. Angel here is actually a big sweetheart," said Regan. The two red-haired siblings gaped at the dragons. Then they spotted Nyx, his massive horns shining in the sunlight.

"Tenebris," the Pride leaders whispered in awe. They turned to Regan, amazement written on their faces.

"There is no way he is tame," declared Ann.

"He is. Nyx!" Regan called. The huge dragon bounded over, his long legs carrying him quickly to Regan's side. He shoved his head into Regan's open hand, which she then scratched.

"But that's impossible! No known dragon has ever been tamed, let alone a Tenebris," said Brian.

"Why do you keep calling him Tenebris?" asked Emma. The two Pride leaders exchanged glances.

"Tenebris is a breed of dragons that control darkness and light. They are the most ferocious kind of dragon, and the biggest. They are said to be the kings and queens of all dragons," said Ann. Regan was shocked.

"Nyx isn't fierce at all! Besides, I've never seen him do anything with light or darkness. How are you so sure he is a Tenebris?" asked Regan.

"Nyx has the Tenebris horns, and notice how, even though he is only nine months old, he is still huge?" Brian said.

"Is he going to keep growing?" asked Katie fearfully.

"Most likely, yes," Ann replied. Nyx snorted.

"Still, we can't be sure he is one of these dragons until he shows his powers, right?" Rya asked.

"He's showing them right now!' exclaimed Emma. Sure enough, Nyx had tendrils of what looked like black smoke twirling around him.

Great timing, Regan thought. Maybe now the Pride leaders would trust them.

"All this talk about our friends here is boring me," she said, hoping one of her friends would agree. Instead, she got the opposite reaction.

"I think it's fun! What breed are the other dragons?" Rya said. Ann looked thoughtful.

"I'd say the green and red are drakes, however the red one is a flame drake, while I believe that the green's powers have something to do with nature."

"What about Angel?" asked Katie.

"A dragonet. Dragonets are the smallest dragons. She probably controls some sort of ice or snow. With dragons you can tell what type of magic they have based on the color of their scales," Brian told them. Katie looked at the white dragon affectionately.

"Where do you guys live?" asked Regan, desperately trying to change the subject. She needed to know more about the Pride before she could trust it or its leaders. Ann looked at her suspiciously, but Brian seemed to buy it.

"That tunnel you see leads to an underground base. It was dug by our ancestors. It has been the home of the Pride ever since."

"Doesn't it get dirty down there, you know, with a soil roof?" asked Emma. Brian shook his head.

"Once you enter it becomes stone, although there are a few dirt patches. We use them for growing plants and vegetables."

"Do you happen to grow this one?" Emma pulled one of the potatoes Katie had found out of the pocket of her thin, gray jacket.

"Actually, yes. We call them solanums," he answered. Emma pulled out one of the coconut-like fruits and looked at him questioningly.

"Cocoe."

"What about these?" Katie asked, pointing at a bush of the sour tasting pink berries Regan had encountered on their first mission for food.

"Those are roseas. Not the best for eating, but they do make good dyes."

"How big are your gardens?" asked Emma, being a gardener herself. For as long as Regan had known her, she'd always been big about plants.

"Why don't we show you?" suggested Ann. Yes, Regan thought. Now she could get a picture of what the Pride's base looked like. The red-haired girl led the way down into the tunnel. As Regan's eyes adjusted to the dim light, she could see lots of people walking around. Most carried torches, while a few carried flashlights.

"If you have flashlights why isn't everyone carrying them instead of torches? They are much safer, aren't they?" asked Regan.

"We only have a few, which are used by the higher ranking Pride members," Ann answered.

"Why don't you just make more?" asked Katie.

"We don't know how," said Brian. He glanced at Ann questioningly. She shook her head at him.

I wonder what that was about, she thought.

"Then how did you get them?" Emma asked.

Ann replied cautiously, "We found them."

"She means they stole them from our house," Regan whispered to Rya, careful not to let the two siblings hear her. Rya nodded slightly, and turned to tell Emma and Katie about Regan's suspicions.

"Well, seeing that it's getting late, we should be going," Regan stated. Ann nodded.

"Do feel free to come back tomorrow! We'd love to get to know more about you, including where you come from. Earth, you called it?"

"Yeah, we would like to learn about how you live as well. Maybe you have some things that could help us," said Emma. Regan could tell that she was thinking about the massive gardens Brian had told them about.

"We would love to tell you about how we live," Brian told them. The short, muscular boy escorted them out of the tunnel and back into the open air. The sun's rays were fading, leaving the surface of the planet in darkness.

"Tomorrow then?" asked Katie.

"We can come back tomorrow if you want," Regan replied.

"Yes!" exclaimed Rya, her blue eyes sparkling with excitement. The four girls mounted their dragons. Katie with an extra boost from Emma.

"King of dragons, huh? You don't seem that royal to me," Regan said to Nyx with affection. He snorted gruffly.

"Alright, alright," she laughed, "let's go home." The mighty dragon took off with a powerful beat of his wings, the other dragons following.

"Hey, is anyone else freezing?" Katie asked. Her arms were wrapped around her tightly and her teeth chattered.

"I'm sweating. Ember's fire power is really hot," said Emma.

"He must not know how to control it yet," suggested Regan. Emma nodded.

"Makes sense."

"Hey, Katie, what if Angel's magic is coming through? You remember what Ann and Brian said, about hers probably having something to do with ice?" Emma pointed out.

"I think you're right. I hope she learns to control it soon, otherwise flying will be miserable," Katie said.

"You won't have to deal with it much longer, I can see the house," Rya told her. Katie sighed in relief. The flight was rather short, now that they knew where they were going.

"Oh, thank you," Katie breathed as they landed next to their gray home. She slid quickly off Angel's back and unhooked her box. As she removed the contraption, Regan could see a layer of frost that was developing on the white dragon's back.

"You were sitting on that?" Rya asked in disbelief. Katie nodded.

"No wonder you were cold!" exclaimed Emma, "Let's go get you warmed up." She led the way back into the house. The dragons flew back to their nest and ate from the massive kill pile they had acquired. Regan thought it was kind of gross how they just dumped all the dead animals into a pile, but dragons were wild creatures too, with wild behaviors. Besides, it was convenient to just walk outside and have multiple choices for dinner. Rya's voice fussing over Katie brought Regan back to the present.

"I'll go get some blankets, Rya, help her to the couch. Emma, could you make something warm for her to eat?" Regan said. The girls did as they were told, each wanting to help Katie as best they could. Regan ran to the bedroom and took all of Katie's blankets off her bed. There were four in total. It was rather hard to walk with the bulky things, but she managed. When she reentered the living room, Katie was lying on the couch with a bowl of soup in her hands. She was shivering even harder than she had been earlier, and her lips were starting to turn blue.

"T-thank y-you," she stammered as Regan gave her the blankets. Her teeth were chattering so hard she could barely talk.

"What if she has hypothermia?" Emma asked worriedly. Katie's face was getting pale, and the small girl huddled closer to Rya for warmth.

"I don't know," she answered truthfully. Regan had never had anything even close to hypothermia, and she had no idea how to treat it other than to keep the person warm.

"I think she does have it," Rya whispered quietly as Katie fell asleep against her. Rya touched her arm. "She's like ice."

"She's breathing slower too," said Emma. Regan was starting to get scared. Then, she remembered a book she'd brought with her.

"Be right back." Regan ran into her bedroom, unzipped her backpack, and grabbed a small survival book out. She flipped to the table of contents and found hypothermia under the topic, *cold*. She rushed back to the living room and showed the page to her friends.

"It says to cover their whole body with blankets and leave only the face clear," read Regan. Rya moved quickly to shift the blankets, leaving only Katie's face exposed.

"She's stopped shivering," observed Emma.

"That may be a sign it's getting worse, according to this," said Regan quickly. She was extremely scared for her friend, who was one of the nicest people she knew.

"It also says to transfer body heat," Rya noted. The three girls unwrapped Katie from the blankets, sat next to her so that they were touching, and then rewrapped the blankets around the four of them.

"What next?" Emma asked hurriedly. Regan shook her head.

"That's it, that's all it says. I mean, other than to give them warm food if they are conscious, but that doesn't help us here." After a few minutes, Katie's breathing quickened and her head lifted.

"What's happening?" she asked groggily.

"You have hypothermia, we are warming you up," Rya told her.

"Had," Regan corrected, "I think the worst of it has passed." Emma sighed in relief.

"That was scary, don't you ever do that to us again!" Emma told her. Katie laughed.

"Sorry, thanks for taking care of me," she said gratefully.

"That's what friends are for. Besides, it's not like we could just let you die. Now eat your soup," Regan told her. Obediently, Katie picked up her spoon and took a bite of the steaming broth.

"That's really good! Where did you find it?" Katie wolfed down the rest of the soup.

"I brought it in a couple days ago. There was a carton of chicken broth in the pantry, hidden in a corner. I don't see how we missed it, but it sure helped in this case," Emma answered. Rya's stomach growled loudly.

"My belly over here is telling me it's my turn to eat," she laughed. Regan stood up slowly and walked out to grab some meat from the dragons. She yawned. It had been a long day, and she was exhausted.

She came back inside with a small part of a bison in her hands. Katie had gotten up and put the blankets away, while Rya and Emma started getting dinner ready. Regan dropped the hunk of meat on the table.

"That big enough?" Emma nodded.

"Yeah, that's plenty big. We are going to make bison mac and cheese," she said. Regan frowned.

"How, when we have no noodles or cheese?"

"Rya here found a large box of noodles in the gym bag she brought, and she also found a cheese wedge in her backpack."

THE PRIDE

"Wow, impressive, Rya," Regan laughed. Rya smiled.

"You never know what you might find in those bags. I was looking for a pair of socks once and found a pizza cutter." Rya chopped up the bison and cooked it on the stove until it was brown. Then she dumped it into a large pot, where Emma was stirring the gooey cheese and noodles.

"I'll set the table," Regan offered. She grabbed the paper plates from one of the wood cabinets and got to work. When she was done, each girl had a fork, spoon, plate, napkin, and glass of water.

"Anyone know where Katie is?" she asked. They shook their heads.

"Haven't seen her since she put those blankets away," Rya told her.

"I'll go look for her while you two finish up." Regan walked to the bedrooms, but didn't see her small friend. Next she looked in the living room. After searching for her fruitlessly in the house, Regan had an idea.

"Maybe she's with Angel." She then went to the dragons' nest, where she found Katie sitting next to the white dragon. Angel no longer had frost covering her, and Katie didn't look cold. Regan went and sat next to Katie.

"I have a bad feeling about the Pride," Katie confessed.

"Why do you say that?" Regan asked, even though she had the same worries. Katie shrugged.

"I don't know. They just kind of send off a bad vibe, I guess," she said. "Does it make me a bad person, that I barely know them and I already think they are bad somehow?" Regan was surprised.

"No, I don't think it does. If you see someone in the streets with a weapon, you're going to think they're up to something bad, right? It doesn't make you a bad person. Besides, I can't even imagine you doing anything mean or bad! You're the nicest person I know!" This seemed to reassure Katie.

"Well, I did steal my brother's teddy bear once," she admitted sheepishly. Regan smiled.

"That's a sibling. It's different. Siblings are supposed to be annoying, right?"

Katie laughed, "Yeah, you're right."

"C'mon, let's go eat." Regan stood up and held out her hand to help Katie up. Katie took it gratefully.

They walked into the house to find Rya and Emma already eating. They halted as they caught sight of Katie and Regan. Regan laughed.

"Well, someone was hungry." Rya averted her eyes from Regan's teasing stare.

"We weren't sure when you were coming back, so we decided to eat while it was still warm," she muttered. Emma nodded quickly in agreement. Grabbing a fork, Regan took a bite of the bison mac and cheese.

"Still warm," she said. Rya glanced at her guiltily.

"I'm sorry, ok? I was starving!"

Regan chuckled, "Just messing with you. I'm hungry, too." She sat down, her long legs cramped under the small table.

"Is it just me, or do you guys have a bad feeling about the Pride?" Regan asked. Emma nodded, while Rya just shook her head and shrugged.

"They seem nice to me," Rya said.

"Everyone seems nice to you," Emma teased, her blue eyes sparkling with amusement.

"Not everyone," smiled Rya. The blond-haired girl took well to teasing, especially when she knew what the person was saying was somewhat true.

"What do you think, Em?" Regan asked, using her friend's old nickname from middle school.

"They seem to want to know a lot about where we came from. Now, that could mean they are very curious people, or that they are planning something that has to do with Earth. They could have bad intentions, but I think we ought to get to know them a little more before we start coming to conclusions," said Emma thoughtfully. Regan nodded.

"Makes sense."

"Yeah," Rya agreed.

"How about this, tomorrow we go over there, if Katie is up to it, and we learn everything we can about them? After that we can see where we stand on things," suggested Regan.

"We have to make sure we don't give them very much information about Earth, just in case," stated Emma.

Rya started, "But-"

"That includes you too, Rya," Regan interrupted, "we can't have them knowing too much. What if they turn out to be bad?"

"Okay," Rya mumbled. The young girl was very talkative, which was why Emma had singled her out for not exposing too many things.

"I'm up for it, if that's what you think we should do," Katie said.

"It's probably our best option right now," said Emma.

"Okay, it's decided. Tomorrow we go over there and find out as much as we can about them," said Regan. The discussion lasted the whole meal. The girls cleaned their plates and got ready for bed.

"Goodnight everyone!" Rya whispered loudly when the lights were turned off. As Regan was about to respond, she saw light coming from Emma's screened off part of the room. She got out of bed and walked over to her friend's room to see what the light was coming from. When she rounded the corner, she saw a flashlight sitting on the bed. Her pale friend was sitting next to the lamp, a pencil in one hand and a large notepad in the other.

"What are you doing?" Regan asked her. Emma jumped, startled.

"When'd you get here?"

"A few seconds ago. Why are you still up?"

Emma replied slowly, "I'm writing letters to my parents and friends."

"And you decided to do this now? Why not do it in daylight, when you can see?" Regan asked. Her friend shrugged.

"I don't know. I guess I was embarrassed by missing them."

Regan sat down next to her. "I miss my family and friends, too. I'm sure Katie and Rya do as well."

"I guess you're right. I just didn't want you to think I was like a child. All of you act so mature," she confessed. Regan snickered.

"You really think Rya is mature?"

Emma laughed quietly, "No, now that I think about it, no."

"She acts like she's three!" Regan whispered, still laughing.

"Yeah," Emma agreed. Regan pointed at the letters.

"Have you thought about how you are going to get those mailed?"

"Actually, yeah. I anticipated missing my parents when I was back on Earth and asked about sending mail. NASA said that there was a tower somewhere that could send it through a satellite or something fancy like that. They said all I had to do was put my letters in through a slot in the wall and it would be sent to them. I've sent one batch of letters already," she told her.

"That sounds cool," Regan said, "Now, if you don't mind, I'm going to sleep. I suggest you do the same. We have a big day tomorrow and you can finish those in the morning."

Emma nodded, "Ok." She turned off the flashlight and put the letters in a pile on the floor next to her bed. "Goodnight, Regan."

"Goodnight, Emma," she replied. Regan hurried back to bed, exhausted after the long day. She was nervous about tomorrow. Who knew what would happen.

Chapter 5

She woke up the next day feeling refreshed and hungry. Katie and Emma woke up at the same time as her, Rya still sleeping heavily.

"Let's make breakfast and surprise her with breakfast in bed," suggested Katie in an excited voice.

"Yeah!" Emma exclaimed loudly.

"Shhh, we don't want to wake her up," Regan whispered. Emma nodded.

"Sorry." The three girls tiptoed into the kitchen, quietly getting out a pan and cutting board. Emma went outside to cut some meat from a pig on the dragons' kill pile. She brought in three long strips of what looked like bacon.

"Looks like bacon, maybe it'll taste the same," she reasoned, laying the meat in the pan. The 'bacon' sizzled, its tasty aroma filling the air.

"Probably not, since there's a whole process for curing it and stuff. But I am amazed at how similar some of the animals here are to the ones back home," Regan said as she flipped the bacon-like meat to its other side.

"Yeah, it's nice having something somewhat familiar in this new world," Emma said, to which Katie agreed.

"That reminds me, where did you put those potato things, Emma? Maybe we could make hash browns," Regan suggested. Katie's face lit up.

"I love hash browns!"

Regan laughed, "I know." Emma pointed to the tiny pantry.

"They're in there. I'll go grab them and get it started. Katie, you could get the tray ready."

"Yes, chef," Katie joked. She rushed to grab a plastic tray from the cabinet. Regan heard her laugh and turned to see her holding a tin tray with a picture of SpongeBob on it. She'd seen it at Rya's house before at one of their many sleepovers.

"Wow, Rya really brought that?" she laughed. Katie smiled.

"I guess. She did say she would marry him when she was younger." This made Regan laugh.

"This bacon is ready," Regan told them, piling a few of the strips onto a paper towel, which was then lifted onto the tin tray. Emma dumped a small stack of hash browns on the tray as well.

"I got her water to drink, let's go see if she is awake," whispered Katie excitedly. The three girls walked quietly to the bedroom, Regan holding the tray. When they came to Rya's room, she was just waking up. Her eyebrows furrowed in confusion as she looked at the tray.

"Surprise!" Katie shouted. Rya pointed at the tray.

"When did you get that?"

"It was in one of the cabinets. Isn't it yours?" asked Regan. Rya nodded.

"Why do you have my SpongeBob?"

Katie smiled, "We made you breakfast in bed!" Rya took the tray happily.

"Oh! Thank you! Sorry I slept in so late," she exclaimed as she shoveled the hash browns into her mouth. Regan, Katie, and Emma had already eaten. Rya cleaned her plate quickly, barely coming up for air in between bites.

"Looks like someone was hungry," Emma teased.

"I was starving!" Rya agreed. When she was finished, Rya climbed out of her bed and threw the bright blue covers onto the floor. "I think it's time we did some laundry."

THE PRIDE

Regan sniffed the blankets. "Yeah, you are definitely right. Those are disgusting!" Her friends laughed.

"We can do some cleaning after we get back from visiting Ann and Brianna," said Emma. Katie glanced at her.

"You mean Brian?" Regan corrected.

"Oh yeah, that was his name! Sorry, I have a cousin named Brianna," Emma explained.

"Anyway, what time are we leaving?" Katie asked as she gathered up the blankets and dumped them into a corner.

"As soon as everyone is ready we can go," Regan answered, walking out of the room. She wanted to grab a few things before they left, including the notepad and pen, her multitool, a gray hoodie, and a small rope. She also took a tiny gadget her dad had bought from a store that sold spy gear. Her dad was a hoarder, yet he never admitted it. She had stolen a few things before she left for Vulcan, including the thing she was holding now. It was a tiny, wireless camera. The outside of the camera was covered in translucent plates, tinted gray. The plates allowed for the camera to camouflage itself, making it invisible to everyone around it except the person who had placed it. She tucked the camera in her pocket, not wanting her friends to know what she was doing. They would frown upon her spying on the Pride leaders, but Regan had to know if they could trust them.

As she turned to leave the room, her backpack slung across her shoulders, Regan noticed a bottle of pills lying on the ground. She bent to pick it up, and, reading the label, figured out that the pills were used to increase hearing immensely. It was another thing she had stolen from her dad's stash.

"Couldn't hurt," she said to herself, shoving the bottle into her other pocket. She slid on her favorite shoes, a pair of black combat boots, and went to meet her friends in the living room.

"Where's Rya?" The blond girl was the only one not in the living room. Katie and Emma were both holding their backpacks.

"She is grabbing a snack." Emma pointed to the kitchen. Rya emerged holding a large box of goldfish.

"Ok, I'm ready now," she said as she stuffed the box into her backpack, which was a light teal color and had her name printed on it in bright orange letters. The box was so big you could see the outline of it bulging through the thick fabric.

"Was there no possible way you could have brought something smaller?" Katie asked.

Rya shook her head, "I don't want to go hungry! What would you do if I starved to death while we were out there?"

"I'm sure you could eat your little frog friend," Regan teased, pointing at a small, spotted frog in the side pocket of Rya's backpack. It jumped out onto the floor, hopping to the door.

"Eat Jeremiah?! No way!" Rya exclaimed in disbelief as she hurried to grab the scrambling frog. Regan laughed.

"Only joking."

"Mostly," Katie added, too quietly for Rya to hear. Katie hated frogs.

"Can we go now?" asked Emma impatiently. Regan nodded and headed to the door, Emma trailing behind her. Katie followed them, staying as far away from the frog as possible. As soon as she was out the door, Jeremiah hopped out behind her. He was quickly snatched up by a bird and flown off.

"No! Jeremiah!" Rya shouted sadly. She quickly brightened, however, as they approached the dragons' nest.

"I've been wondering this, but how do you think they ended up here? I mean, they can't have just magically appeared, right?" Emma wondered aloud as she climbed onto Ember's back. Regan had just been wondering the same thing.

"Do you think NASA sent them?" suggested Rya. Katie shook her head in disagreement.

"No, if they had, we would have known." Katie climbed onto Angel's back, and Regan noticed she hadn't strapped on the box she had made for her. Katie saw her looking at her.

"I'm not scared anymore. I trust Angel," she said calmly. Regan smiled at her.

"Good, there's nothing to be scared of." Regan was already sitting on Nyx's back, holding on to his massive horns. "Everyone ready?"

"Yep," Rya replied.

"All set!" shouted Emma. Rya didn't wait for Katie's reply, but took off quickly. Nakata's wings sent a gust of air through the nest, rustling the sticks that made up the nest. Ember and Angel followed the giant green dragon. Regan and Nyx were last. The black dragon's wings were almost touching the sides of the nest when he spread them. Regan could tell he had grown as they flew after the other three dragons. He seemed to have gotten stronger as well. He didn't have to beat his wings as much to keep flying, but rather seemed to glide after each flap. The other dragons were just as graceful, flying soundlessly through the dawn light. Their scales glinted in the sun.

It didn't take long for the four girls to reach the entrance to the Pride's underground base. They landed softly next to the tunnel. Regan slid off Nyx's back and patted him on the neck.

"That was awesome!" Katie exclaimed. Angel let her wing rest on the ground, acting as a slide for Katie to dismount. Once Katie was off, she hugged the dragonet. Frost was beginning to form on the white dragon's head.

"Not fair. How come all your dragons have shown their powers but not mine?" Rya huffed. The green dragon must have heard her, because when she went to slide off she bucked, causing Rya to go flying into Emma, who was just getting off.

"Hey!" exclaimed Emma. The impact sent both girls sprawling onto the ground. Rya was first to stand up, dusting off her clothes and glaring at Nakata. Meanwhile, Katie was laughing hysterically. Regan tried to hide her smile, knowing it would only make Rya angrier.

"That was rude," Rya said to the dragon, who snorted loudly. Rya offered a hand to Emma grumpily. Emma took it gratefully. After she stood up, Emma dusted off her clothes and headed for the tunnel.

Someone's in a hurry, thought Regan silently. She followed her friend, Katie and Rya close behind. She checked her pockets, making sure she still had the camera and hearing pills. When they reached the entrance, Regan gestured for Rya and Katie to go in first. The second their backs were turned she popped one of the tiny, white hearing pills into her mouth and swallowed it. Regan shoved the bottle back into her pocket and hurried after her friends.

Her friends weren't that far ahead. When she caught up with them, Katie glanced at her, but said nothing. The tunnel widened out into the same stone cavern it had last time, yet as she looked around, Regan noticed that there weren't any people around. Torches hung from the walls in sconces, illuminating the cave with a warm light.

"Anyone have a flashlight?" asked Emma, gazing around at their surroundings.

"We don't need one," answered Rya as she yanked one of the torches from the wall. It sent a shower of sparks around her, yet somehow she avoided the flames.

"I mean, it works," said Katie cheerfully as she skipped through the darkness behind Rya, who was leading the way to another large cavern. It was lit dimly as was the cave they were in, but Regan could just make out the shapes of people. She quickened her pace. As she got closer, she could hear the voices of Ann and Brian. It seemed to be coming from a small cave to the left, not the main one they were heading towards.

"There's Ann and Brian," she stated. Emma glanced at her, confused.

"What do you mean? I can't see anything."

Regan pointed to the cave. "Over there. Can't you hear them?"

"No," Rya said. She didn't question though, and veered to the left, heading for Ann and Brian. It was then Regan realized she could hear them because of the pills she had taken.

They work! she thought excitedly. The hollow wasn't far, and they reached it just as Ann and Brian walked out, each holding red flashlights that glowed. Ann looked surprised as the light from her flashlight shone on the four girls. Brian jumped, startled.

"Sorry, we couldn't see anyone near the tunnel, so we kinda let ourselves in," Katie said apologetically. Ann smiled, but it didn't quite reach her eyes.

"It's alright. We were just talking about you, in fact. What brings you here?" Brian asked brightly.

"Well, you said we could come back today to learn about, what's it called again?" Rya fumbled for the word.

"The Pride," finished Emma, Rya smiling at her gratefully. Brian laughed.

"Yep, anything you want to know," he said, still smiling.

"Well, first of all, how did your ancestors end up here?" Regan started.

"Before you ask questions, why don't we go to our office?" Ann suggested, turning back toward the large wooden door embedded in the stone. She opened the door, Brian following her. Rya went in eagerly, Emma and Katie right behind her. When Regan hesitated, Rya grabbed her arm and dragged her in. The room was spacious and brightly lit with torches. In the middle was a large desk, and behind it a swivel chair. Covering the floor was a huge red and gold area rug, something that royalty might own.

"Woah," whispered Emma in awe. Katie nodded, gaping at the walls, which were covered in paintings of people. All of them had the same red hair and smiling mouths. Ann sat down in the chair and let the girls look around for a bit.

"Who are the people in the paintings?" asked Emma, who was examining the pictures closely.

"Our ancestors," Brian replied. He gestured to a large painting of a man and woman. "Those are our parents, Wendy and John." The last words he choked out, his eyes watering. Ann's head was down, but Regan could see a single tear roll down her cheek. The red-haired girl wiped it away and looked up, trying to hide her sadness.

"So, um, how did you guys get here? On Vulcan, I mean," asked Rya, desperately trying to lighten the mood.

"You want to know how our ancestors got here?" asked Brian. Rya nodded in confirmation. "Well, they originally came from where you came from, Earth. They were sent to Mars when people were first trying to colonize it. But their rocket was sent off course when it was hit by an asteroid. They crash landed here, along with all the animals they'd brought with them."

Ann gestured toward a caged animal near the back of the room, next to a small bookcase. When Regan got closer, she saw that it resembled an iguana. The only difference was that the scales were dull red instead of green.

"The animals adapted, changing the color of their scales, their fur. The only animals that were here before were the dragons," Brian told them, "The fiercest was known as the Tenebris breed. They attacked the people constantly. It was only when the dragons discovered the animals that they left the people alone."

"How do you know all this? It was a long time ago, right?" Katie inquired. Ann pointed toward the bookcase where Regan was standing. "They wrote everything that happened down in their journals, which were handed down through the years."

"How often do you read them?" asked Regan. She needed to know where to place the camera, and the bookcase had a perfect view of everything in the room. Ann narrowed her eyes.

"Once every year we have a ceremony to remember our history, we read them then," she answered cautiously. *Dang it, why'd you have to ask that?* Regan berated herself silently. She couldn't hide the camera there now, it was too obvious.

"Anyway, enough about us. Let's talk about you," Ann said, smiling.

"How did you get here?" Brian asked.

Rya replied, "Well, we flew here on dragons, duh." Ann rolled her eyes.

"He means how did you get to Vulcan."

"You know, that makes more sense," she laughed. While Ann and Brian were distracted, Regan slipped behind the desk to the other side of the room. There was a statue of a dragon tucked into the corner. Its mouth was open, its long fangs bared in a silent roar. The wings were spread out as if it were to take off and fly. The dragon stood on its hind legs, his front legs in a pose that reminded Regan of a T-Rex. She heard Ann ask Emma another question, this one about how the governments on Earth operated. She grabbed the camera out of her pocket and knelt down, trying to act like she was looking at the dragon's teeth. She wedged the camera in between its fangs, the camera changing colors to blend in with the rough gray stone. Slowly, she stood up and turned around to face her friends and the Pride leaders, who were engrossed in their conversation about the underground base. Hiding the camera had taken about two minutes.

Katie was speaking, "So you dug this whole thing?"

"No, most of it was a natural cave, we just modified it a little." Brian said.

"That's so cool!" Rya said brightly. Ann stood up from her chair, waving toward the door.

"Would you like a tour?"

Rya jumped. "Heck yeah!" Brian led the way out the door, Katie skipping behind him. Emma and Rya went next, following the red-haired boy back out into the main cavern and into the larger one they had been heading toward earlier. Ann went last, making sure Regan was in front of her before she left the room. This made Regan suspicious, but she said nothing as they made their way toward the large cave.

When they walked into the cavern, Regan could see that there were many people eating at various stone tables strewn about the room. It was chaotic, yet at the same time orderly. *Interesting,* she thought. Brian walked up to a man in a white uniform, standing erect next to a metal door. The man's red hair was cropped short, and his eyes were a dark brown. Brian had a quick conversation with him, pointing at the four girls. The man nodded and walked over to them. As Regan was watching, another man came to take his spot, dressed in the same white uniform.

"That guy is freaky," Rya said to her under her breath.

"No kidding," she whispered back. Katie's eyes were wide, and Regan noticed her hands were shaking. Emma glanced at her, and Regan nodded toward Katie. Emma went to stand next to Katie, and the small girl looked up at her gratefully.

"This is Wesley, our head of security," Ann introduced. The big man nodded in greeting.

"Does he talk?" asked Rya. Brian smiled.

"Not much, no."

"Why do you need security? Aren't you the only people here?" Emma inquired. Ann shook her head.

"We have a set of rules, Wesley and the guards are here to enforce them."

Katie raised her hand, an old habit from school, "What type of rules?"

"Every morning we gather in the Great Hall and recite the Pledge of Obedience and Loyalty. We also have set meeting times, among other things," Brian told them. Brian and Ann were then called away by an important looking officer

"I'm sorry, there's something wrong with the security cameras. We have to go check it out. It won't take long, but feel free to explore until we come back," Ann said as she headed toward the metal door Wesley had been protecting earlier.

"Why don't we ask some of the people about these rules? Something feels off," Regan suggested to her friends. Emma nodded.

"I agree, let's see what we can find out," Rya agreed. Regan and Rya headed for a family eating near the back of the room. The couple had two kids, a boy and a girl. The woman looked up when they approached, and her eyes widened. She nudged her husband, who then glanced up at the approaching two girls as well. When they got to the table, Rya sat down first and smiled warmly.

"Hey, guys, I'm Rya, and this is Regan. What's your name?" The question was aimed at the woman, who was staring at her, apprehension written on her face.

"Amanda," she answered quietly. She took another bite of the food, which was a bowl of plain noodles and chicken broth.

Rya was not discouraged by the short response, however. "So we've heard there is a set of rules here, could you tell us about them?" At this Amanda looked truly terrified. She looked around warily, making sure no one was around. Then, she spoke in a very soft voice.

"The High Ones control us, who we marry, when we go to sleep, when we eat. We can only have two children. Every morning we must pledge loyalty to them."

"High Ones?" Regan inquired. The man answered this time.

"Ann and Brian." He spat the names, glaring at the door the two siblings had disappeared through.

"Why don't you stop them? Why follow them?" Regan asked, keeping her voice to a whisper.

"The guards," the man said, "they haul away anyone who speaks badly of the High Ones. Anyone who looks different gets taken too. The ones they take, don't come back." Horrified, Regan thanked the couple and hurried away, Rya not far behind. They met up with Emma and Katie in the middle of the room.

"We got nothing," Emma told them. Regan and Rya shared a glance.

"I assume you guys found something?" Katie concluded. Rya nodded grimly.

"Let's not talk about it here," Regan said quietly, as Ann and Brian approached.

"Now that the security is fixed, would you like a tour of the base?" Brian offered. Emma went to accept, but Regan interrupted her before she could finish.

"It's getting late, we should really get going."

Ann's eyebrows furrowed. "It's noon?"

"Exactly, late. It was very nice meeting with you. We can show ourselves out." Regan nudged Katie toward the door.

"Oh no, we wouldn't want to be rude. We'll send you with an escort. You don't want to get hurt, do you?" Ann asked. Her smile was that of a viper, full of barely concealed venom.

"No, I guess not." she conceded, her voice shaking slightly. Ann snapped her fingers and five guards, all in the same white uniform, came rushing forward. All of them were huge, hands as big as hams.

As they were ushered out, Regan took a good look at her surroundings. Now that she knew about the high security, she noticed small cameras tucked into the walls. It didn't take long for them to get out of the base. Regan squinted against the glaring sunlight after being pushed outside. Rya whistled loudly, and Nakata flew in with a loud whoosh, followed by Nyx, Ember, and Angel.

"Let's get out of here," Regan urged. She rushed up to Nyx and climbed onto his back smoothly, Rya following suit.

"Why are you two in such a hurry?" Emma asked.

"Those rules, they are really, really bad," Rya explained hurriedly. Katie, catching on to Rya and Regan's fear, began shaking slightly.

"We can talk about it at the house," Regan added. Nyx took off with a loud beating of his wings, the other three dragons following close behind. They flew back to the house in silence, Regan occasionally glancing behind her for fear of being followed. *This is stupid,* she thought. *We have no reason to be afraid of them, just because they have some extreme rules. Heck, the rules don't even apply to us!* However, as much as she tried to convince herself that everything was fine, she couldn't shake the feeling that something bad was happening, and they were stuck in the middle of it.

As soon as Regan caught a glimpse of their home, she let out a sigh of relief. The dragons landed next to their nest loudly, stomping and snorting. Regan slid off Nyx's back, his wings drooping onto the ground. The large dragon lifted his wings slowly, flying unsteadily into the nest, where he dropped with a thud, immediately falling asleep among the sticks and mattresses.

Regan waited for her friends to get off their dragons and then the four girls walked together to the house in silence. She opened the door and motioned for them to sit in the living room.

"Okay, so what is this all about? Rushing home? Those guards? Why?" Katie suddenly exploded. The other three were shocked. Rarely ever did Katie lose her temper like this. Rya and Regan explained what they had found out from Amanda and her husband. When they were finished, both Katie and Emma were speechless.

"Yeah, I'm afraid Ann knows that we know about the rules, and that's why she sent the guards to take us out," Rya confessed, chewing her lip. Then, Regan remembered the camera she'd hidden in Ann's office. She was still a little wary about telling her friends, but now was as good a time as any.

"Um, guys, I may or may not have hid a camera in Ann's office while we were there." She looked down at her hands.

"So that's what you were doing in there," Rya realized.

"Regan, that was genius!" Emma exclaimed, hugging the surprised girl tightly. "Why didn't you tell us? I would've helped you hide it!"

"I was scared you'd be mad at me," she answered sheepishly.

"Well, we're not, right guys?" Emma prompted.

"Yeah! I definitely would've helped hide that thing!" Rya laughed.

"Me too! How'd you even get a camera? It must've been small because neither of them spotted it, not to mention us," Katie asked curiously. Regan laughed.

"My dad's a hoarder and he had them in his collection of stuff. I stole it from him before we left Earth, along with these." She pulled out the bottle of hearing pills.

"And that's how you heard where they were when we first came in," Emma finished when she read the label.

"So what are we gonna do about Ann and Brian?" asked Katie.

"What do you mean 'what are we gonna do?'" Rya's eyebrows furrowed, "There's nothing we can do."

"Well, we can't just leave those people to live like that!" argued Regan, crossing her arms.

"True," she agreed. Regan leaned back in her chair, her mouth set. What could they do?

"How about we start with something simple, say the camera. Can we look at the recording live?" prompted Emma, the question directed at Regan.

She shrugged. "I have my phone connected to it, but I'm not sure if it'll work without wifi."

"It'll work," Rya replied confidently.

"How can you be sure?" Regan, having never worked with any type of security camera before, had no idea that there were cameras made to work without Wi-Fi.

"Because at my house there wasn't any internet, so our security cameras had to go without it." Rya had grown up on a farm, and the others had been over so many times that they knew about the internet. The cameras, however, were new to Regan.

"Wait, you had security cameras?" she asked, raising her eyebrows. Rya nodded. "I didn't think your family was big on that type of stuff."

"My dad decided it was a good idea after my aunt's house got robbed," she explained, "I never really got the point. We live in the country, no one's going to rob a farm."

"Good point." Emma shifted her gaze to Regan. "Are you going to show us the footage or not?"

"Right." Regan pulled out her phone, a small device in a black case. The phone set off a light glow in the dim room. She scrolled to the app she used to connect it to the camera and tapped on it. She had to sign in using her dad's email address, as it was his camera.

"Alright, here it is," she announced, pulling up the recording. It happened to be live, and Ann and Brian were sitting behind the big desk in the office, facing a man they had never seen before. He was tall compared to the two siblings, and his fiery red hair was shaved close to his head. His eyes were a caramel brown, and he had a big, bushy beard.

"Who's that?" Rya asked. Regan shrugged.

"No idea. Let's find out." The four girls huddled around the small screen. They could faintly hear the three people talking.

"Turn the volume up," Emma told her. She turned it all the way up, making sure everyone could hear it. "Is there a record button? We might need to revisit the footage later." Regan nodded upon seeing a camera button in the right hand corner and tapped it. The button was replaced by a flashing red light.

"I want them kept out of that room," Ann was saying, quite forcefully.

"Yes, High One," the man answered. "Is there anything else I can do for you?"

"Check on the rocket, make sure the construction is going well."

"As you wish, High One." The man bowed, and left the room, shutting the door softly behind him.

"Hector is a good servant," Brian commented as he took a sip of a pink drink.

"Looks like pink lemonade," Rya laughed, bringing Regan's mind back to the living room.

"Shhh," Emma shushed.

"Yes, Mother always said he was one we could trust," Ann acknowledged. Brian nodded.

"I miss her," he said, a tear in his eye.

"Me too. She'd be proud of what we are doing," Ann told him, laying a comforting hand on her brother's shoulder.

"They look so sad," observed Katie softly. "Maybe they don't know that the rules are bad. It's all they've ever known right?"

"Let's just keep listening and find out." Regan propped the phone up on the coffee table so they didn't have to crowd around her.

Brian was now speaking, "Yeah, she always said she'd love to see Earth."

What does he mean, 'see Earth', Regan thought. She soon found out.

"Yes, the rocket was one of her greatest ideas. It will be named in her honor. When we fly it to Earth, I want them all to know her name," Ann declared, her green eyes bright against her sunburned skin. *They can't fly to Earth, the rocket won't work,* Regan tried to convince herself, but to no avail.

"Wait a minute, they're going to Earth. What if they bring their rules there too?" Katie panicked. Regan quickly tried to reassure her.

"Hang on now, they're not going to establish their rules on Earth." Just as she finished speaking, she heard Ann talking and brought her attention back to the screen.

"Once the rightful law is brought to Earth they will be under our control."

"We'll make them regret never going looking for us," Brian said, his eyes sparking with anger. *So much for that.*

"They're going to do it!" Katie was in full panic mode now, her breathing ragged and uneven.

"Slow down, Katie. We won't let that happen," Emma said to her, hugging her friend.

"How?" she squeaked, slipping out of the hug. Rya's eyes gleamed.

"We have to stop them," she said. She glanced at Regan. "And we have to help those people." Regan nodded.

"We'll wreck the rocket." She pointed at the phone, where they could see Ann and Brian walked out the door, probably to check on the rocket themselves. "And somehow we'll find a way to take those two down while we're at it." She ended the recording and slipped the phone into her pocket.

Katie started to calm down a little. "But how are we going to get in that room? It's probably locked." Regan thought about it.

"What if we asked some of the people to help us? You could tell Amanda's husband hated Ann and Brian by the way he spoke about them. There's probably more like him."

"Amanda?" Emma frowned.

"The person we talked to when Ann and Brian were gone," Regan explained. "She and her husband told us about the rules."

"Oh, makes sense." Emma crossed her arms. "So, how are we going to ask people to help us? It's not like we can just waltz in there and say 'oh we are trying to destroy this rocket and bring down your leaders, care to join?'"

"What's a waltz?" Rya asked. Emma shook her head.

"You're missing the point, Rya." Suddenly, Regan remembered something the man had said.

"Hey, remember what the man said, that anyone who says something bad about Ann or Brian gets taken away and doesn't come back?" Katie looked even more terrified, and Regan vaguely remembered leaving that part out when she and Rya told them about the rules.

"You left that part out," the small girl accused. Regan frowned.

"Sorry. Anyway, what if they aren't dead? What if they just get, like, thrown out or something?" she suggested. Emma's eyes brightened.

"Like an outcast?"

Regan nodded, smiling. "Yeah. If we can find them, if there do happen to be outcasts, there's a good chance they'll help us."

"They'll want revenge," said Rya, finally catching on to what the others were thinking.

"Exactly!" Regan exclaimed. Katie hesitated.

"Aren't we grasping at straws here?"

"Huh?" Rya asked. Katie ignored her.

"There's a good chance there are no outcasts. Without them, this plan of destroying the rocket is doomed. If we don't destroy the rocket, Earth is doomed, along with all of our families and friends." She sank down, dropping her head into her hands, hopeless. Rya sat down next to her and hugged her, but Katie shrugged her off. With a pang, Regan thought of her mom and dad, and her two sisters.

"We won't let that happen," she said, determination flooding her mind. She laid a hand on Katie's shoulder. "Even if no one will help us, we'll find a way." Katie looked up at her, her eyes watering. She sniffed and smiled, wiping away her tears.

"Okay." Regan offered her and Rya each a hand and, when they took them, helped pull them up.

"Let's eat something and start searching for some people. Surely they can't be too hard to find, right?" Emma suggested. The four girls ate a quick meal of the leftover hash browns and bacon from breakfast. The food was cold, and the hash browns had gotten mushy while they were sitting in the fridge, and left a stale taste in her mouth.

When they were finished washing dishes they rushed out to the dragons' nest. It was a few hours after noon when Regan passed through the large doorway to the inside of the nest, where the dragons were wrestling. Legs and tails all tangled up, the four beasts kicked and swiped at each other playfully. Ice, vines, flames, and tendrils of darkness wrapped around them, caused by the dragons' now controllable powers. Nyx was the first to hear the crunching of the girls' footsteps on the sticks, and raised his massive head in greeting, his horns glistening under the bright sun. The big animal untangled himself from the rest of the dragons, who were just then noticing the girls. He trotted over to Regan, who scratched his chin affectionately.

"Hey, Nyx," she said, placing her forehead against his. He snorted, and pawed at the ground. She smiled. He seemed to be expecting a flight, and he was right. The girls had decided over lunch to fly around and see if they could spot any people. Gradually, the other dragons came over too.

"Who's a good dragon? Who's a good dragon? You are," Rya told her dragon warmly as she patted it on the neck. Nakata purred and leaned her head into Rya's hand.

"Jeez, Ember! You're hot!" Emma exclaimed, shaking her hand vigorously. Now that she looked closer, Regan could see that the air around the fire dragon was hazy. She remembered the fire at her house on earth, the one they had been using to burn boxes. The air above that had been similar to this.

"Well, he was just using his power," Katie said honestly. Emma gritted her teeth, still shaking her hand.

"Hadn't noticed."

Regan was quick to break up the brewing fight. "Let's not get angry now, she was just stating the facts." Emma glared at her. "Okay, get angry then," she muttered to herself.

"Angel should be pretty cold as well," Rya noted. Regan, seeing the frost beginning to form on the white dragon's scales, nodded.

"Maybe you can cool your hand off on her," she suggested to her friend, whose hand was beginning to turn bright red. She walked over to the small dragon, her blue eyes glittering with annoyance. She laid her hand on Angel's side, sighing as the cold soothed her burn. She took it off before it froze, rubbing it slowly.

"Thanks, Angel," she whispered. Regan smiled.

"Are we good to go now then?" She hopped on to Nyx's back, almost falling short, but catching herself by gripping his scales and pulling herself the rest of the way up. Rya frowned.

"But Ember is still burning hot, and Angel is still freezing?"

Regan scolded herself quietly. "Right. Let's wait for them to get back to normal, then leave." She slid off the huge black dragon. Nyx whined, confused. She rubbed his neck. "Soon, buddy."

"Good idea." Emma sat down on a rather fluffy mattress, sinking down as feathers flew everywhere. Regan laughed.

"Rough day so far?" she asked. Emma glared at her. She sat down on a mattress across from Emma, Rya sitting next to her. Katie sat beside Emma, feathers once again flying as she dropped down on the grey-white bed. They watched as the dragons played, this time without using their powers. They batted at the many bats screeching above their heads and rolled around among the sticks and bedding. Seeing this childish behavior, Regan began to wonder how they had ever thought dragons could be vicious or evil.

When they were done playing, the dragons settled down for a short nap. Nyx trotted over to Regan and Rya, where he promptly flopped down on the bed, sending the two girls flying into the air. They landed back down with a loud thump. Both girls were laughing. Nyx had curled up behind them, forming a sort of backrest. Regan could still see a little bit of his power, in the form of a curtain of darkness covering his eyes when he closed them.

"It's like he's wearing a sleeping mask," Katie whispered, pointing to the covering. Regan nodded, smiling. She leaned back against the enormous dragon, his scales cool despite the blazing sunlight. Eventually, Nakata came over too, laying beside Rya and resting her giant head on her lap. The dragon's bright yellow eyes looked up at her friend affectionately. Rya laid her hand on Nakata's head. Angel and Ember were sleeping a few feet away from them.

After laying there for a while longer, Rya began to drift asleep, Katie following her lead. Pretty soon, Emma's eyes were closed too. Regan, not ever being able to sleep during the day, started reminiscing about her basketball team. She'd played with the team for four years, and had become very close with her teammates. Rya and Emma had been on the team. Katie had joined the last year Regan had played, having moved houses.

Suddenly, she heard a noise. It sounded like footsteps walking on gravel. She knew there were a lot of rocks around the house, and she wondered what the noise was coming from. Quietly, she scooted over to Rya and shook her awake.

"Wha-"

"Shhh, there's something here. Near the house. Let's wake up the others and go see what it is." Rya nodded, and quietly got up and went over to Katie. Regan tiptoed to Emma. Again, she shook her awake, her blue eyes flying open. Regan held up a finger to shush her and gestured for her to follow. She led the way to the door, climbing over the dragons' legs and tails along her way. The four girls walked slowly, trying not to make much noise. When they got to the door, they huddled behind the wall. Regan could still hear the noises, and they seemed to have gotten louder. She also thought she could hear voices whispering. Peeking her head around the corner, she caught a glimpse of two short figures. Both wore red clothes from head to toe. Regan couldn't imagine how they weren't dying from the heat.

As she watched, the form on the left looked over its shoulder, glancing about to make sure no one was looking. Regan thought she saw a pair of bright green eyes, and then the person turned back to what they were doing.

"Who are they?" Rya asked, whispering loudly. Regan shushed her, then quietly answered back.

"I have no idea. I think they might be people. It looks like they're trying to break into the house."

"How many?" Emma inquired.

"Two," she said back. Rya pushed her way up to the front.

"I want to see." Rya nudged Regan roughly, causing her to lose her footing and fall. Crouched as they were, she didn't fall far, but the sound of the gravel shifting under her made a loud noise. Glancing up, Regan saw the two people look their way. Quickly she scooted back behind the wall, pulling Rya with her.

"Great, now what?" she asked, glaring at Rya. Her best friend shrugged.

Emma answered her instead, "Well, we can't just let them steal our stuff can we?" Regan frowned.

"No."

"Wait a minute guys," Katie spoke, her eyes bright. "What if those are the outcasts?!"

Regan answered thoughtfully, "Maybe, but I want to be sure they are before we-"

"Hey, guys!" Rya had rushed out to greet the two people, waving. Swiftly, the red cloaked figures ran off, their clothes swishing around their feet.

"Rya!" Regan scolded. Rya grinned sheepishly at her.

"Sorry."

Emma groaned, "Now we have to go after them."

"Not necessarily," Katie replied, pointing to the dragons, who were lazily batting at flies buzzing around their heads.

Chapter 6

"Ember!" Emma shouted. The drake glanced at her. "Catch them?" She gestured toward the two fleeing figures. Ember nudged the other three dragons and took off, his wings flapping loudly. The others followed suit.

"Don't eat them!" Rya added. Regan glanced at her, and Rya shrugged. "You never know." As they watched, the four dragons split up. Nakata began to fall behind while Angel flew faster, making her way to the front. Nyx and Ember spread to the sides, eventually forming a sort of cross. They passed over the two figures, casting enormous shadows on the people. They looked up just as the dragons landed, surrounding them. Fearfully, the two people glanced around, trying to find a way out, yet finding none. They were trapped.

"Well that went well," Regan commented as Nyx and Nakata picked the people up in their claws and made their way back to the nest. The four girls came out from behind the door and walked to the clearing in front of the dome-like structure. The dragons dropped the two forms before landing with a loud thump, Angel and Ember doing the same.

Finally realizing that the girls were not going to hurt them, the two people took off their hoods, revealing them to be boys who looked to be about their age. Funny how everyone seemed to be so young. One was tall, had darker skin, and brown eyes, while the second was shorter, pale, and had blue eyes. Both were dark haired and seemed angry at being caught.

"What do you want?" the tall one asked in a gruff voice.

"More like, what do *you* want? You were the ones trying to break into our house," Regan pointed out.

"We weren't breaking in, the door was unlocked," replied the short one. Emma rolled her eyes.

"If you weren't trying to steal something, what were you doing?" Katie asked. The two boys glanced at each other, and finally the taller one spoke.

"We never said we weren't trying to steal something," he grinned.

"What were you stealing then?" Regan pried. It didn't take long for the taller boy to answer.

"Food," he admitted. "We were running short at camp and most of the hunters are sick, so we thought to help out we would find some." He kicked at a pebble awkwardly.

"Hold up, camp? Hunters?" Emma was frowning. The shorter boy was quick to answer.

"Camp of Outcasts. The hunters kill prey for us to eat, but we were struck by some sort of virus or something. They cough and sneeze a lot." Suddenly, he smiled. "I'm Lucas by the way. And this is Ace." He pointed to his friend, who slapped his hand away.

Ace whispered to Lucas, "Too much information. We don't know if we can trust these people. Let's get out of here." Regan overheard it, however, as Ace was quite loud when he spoke.

"You can trust us," she assured him. He glanced at her, unsure.

"Yeah, we were just going to go looking for people like you. Outcasts," Emma added. "You were part of the Pride once, right?"

Ace nodded.

"It was awful," the big boy shuddered.

"Don't you want to help the people still living there?" Rya asked, encouragingly. Both boys nodded.

"We do, too. The Pride leaders, Ann and Brian, are planning to launch a rocket that will land on Earth, our home planet. They want to invade it and establish their rules there too," Regan explained quickly. Lucas's eyes lit up.

"Ace, this is our chance to show everyone we aren't little kids anymore!"

Ace, however, looked doubtful. "How do we know we can trust you? It's not like you have proof of these guys saying this."

"Actually, we do. Come inside and we'll show you." Katie waved them over to the house, where they gathered in the living room to watch the clip. Pulling her phone out of her pocket, Regan went into the camera app and went to replay the recording of the two leaders.

"What's that?" Ace asked, pointing to the device. Regan suddenly realized they probably hadn't seen a phone before.

"It's called a phone. You can use it for all sorts of things, like taking pictures, videos, or calling someone."

"What do you mean by call?" Lucas asked.

"Well, I can't show you since we don't have internet or wifi here..."

"The stuff you need to make it work," Emma interjected. Regan nodded.

"Right, you need those to make calls, but basically when you call somebody, you can hear them when they talk, even if they're really far away."

"Cool!" Ace smiled. "Maybe when you get some of that internet stuff you can show us?"

"Sure." Regan grinned back at him. It caught her off guard when they said they didn't know what a phone was, but it made sense. How would they have access to such a device on an unknown planet?

When the short explanation was over, Regan played the video.

"Wow," Lucas said bluntly after they finished watching it. Regan nodded.

"So will you help us?" she asked hopefully. The two boys shared a look, and then Ace answered.

"We will, but we can't speak for the rest of the people at camp."

Katie glanced at Regan, who shrugged. "It's a start."

"Do you think we could talk to your campmates?" Emma asked.

Lucas nodded. "Yeah, we can take you there. It's a long walk from here to there though."

Regan smiled. "We won't be walking." The boys looked confused for a moment, until Emma gestured outside to the dragons, who were flying above the nest, playing. Lucas's eyes widened.

"You ride those things?" Rya nodded in excitement.

"Yeah! The green one's mine," she answered proudly. Regan laughed.

"You two can ride with us so it doesn't take as long. It's getting late and I personally want to be home before it gets dark. Who knows what sort of things are out there," Emma told them. They followed the blond girl out to the nest. The dragons saw them coming and soared over to them, dropping down with a loud thump.

"Yes ma'am!" Lucas saluted jokingly. Emma glared at him, Rya and Regan snickering behind her back.

"One of them can ride with me; Nakata is big enough," Rya offered.

"Nyx can take two people too," Regan added.

"Who is Nyx?" Lucas asked, his eyes glancing over the four dragons excitedly. She pointed to Nyx, his black wings raised against the slowly darkening sky. His scales gleamed in the dim light. Ace's eyes lit up.

"I call riding the big one!" he exclaimed. Lucas looked disappointed, but brightened up when he saw Nakata.

"Are we leaving or not?" Emma asked, her voice impatient. She was already sitting on Ember's back, waiting for the others to do the same. Rya boosted Lucas up on Nakata's back, and helped Regan do the same with Ace.

"Hey, what do we hold on to up here?" Ace called down to them. He was wobbling quite a lot, and Regan couldn't imagine him staying on the dragon when they took off.

"He is not holding on to me." Rya gestured to Lucas, who looked offended. "Gross."

"Hey! I'm not that bad!" he yelled back. Rya ignored him. Katie, who was quiet for the whole ordeal, spoke up and shared her idea.

"What if we made some sort of reins for them and tied it around the dragons' bellies or something?"

"Not a bad idea," Regan acknowledged. "But how are we going to make that long of a rope right now?"

"Why do we need to make it fast?" Rya asked her. She pointed at Emma, who was glaring off into the distance at an erupting volcano.

"So we don't make Miss Grumpy Pants even madder," she explained quietly.

"Oh, makes sense." Rya's eyebrows furrowed thoughtfully, then she turned to Nakata. The dragon was waiting patiently for Rya to mount. Lucas waved at the two girls, but both ignored him, again.

"What if we don't make them?" Katie inquired. Regan turned to glance at her.

"What do you mean?"

Katie pointed to Nakata. "She has nature powers, right?"

"She does?" Ace interrupted. Katie glared at him, and continued talking.

"Well, what if we just ask her to make a really long vine?"

Regan smiled, "You are just full of great ideas tonight aren't you?" Katie beamed at the compliment. "Rya, ask Nakata to make a really long vine."

"How long is really long?"

"Long enough to fit around her whole body. C'mon Rya, think about it. We were just talking about what we were using it for," Regan laughed. Rya smiled.

"Right," she replied. She whistled to Nakata, who looked at her attentively. "HEY GIRL, YOU THINK YOU CAN MAKE A REALLY REALLY LONG ROPE FOR US?" she screamed at the dragon.

"YOU TALKING TO ME?" Lucas yelled back in a confused voice. Rya shook her head and pointed at Nakata.

"ARE YOU A GIRL?" Regan asked Lucas snarkily.

"Do you think you guys can stop screaming, it's hurting my ears," Emma said grumpily.

"SURE THING!" Rya yelled up to her friend, who glared at her and resumed watching the volcano, muttering under her breath. Regan laughed.

"Hey, look! She's doing it!" Katie exclaimed, pointing to the large, green dragon. Indeed, Regan could make out two small vines appearing from the dragon's nostrils.

"Odd place to grow a vine," she laughed. Lucas and Rya were both dying laughing at the sight, and Nakata huffed, annoyed. She did as asked, however, and produced two extremely long vines that easily made it all the way around her body.

"Those two are going to be good friends," Regan commented to Katie, gesturing at Lucas and Rya. Katie nodded.

"Totally."

As Regan walked over to Nakata, she realized they had nothing to cut the vines with. She remembered Emma telling her she always carried a pocket knife, and turned to the blond haired girl.

"Emma, can I borrow your pocket knife?" she asked loudly. Without looking at her, Emma tossed the knife down. It landed at her feet, a shiny blade with a dark brown handle. She picked it up, dusted it off, and tossed it to Rya. Nakata had lowered her head so Rya could reach the vines, and Rya was standing next to her waiting patiently. She caught the knife with ease, and began sawing at the vine viciously.

"Shouldn't you be more careful with that knife?" Ace asked. Rya laughed.

"Us, careful? No way."

"It was closed when we threw it," Regan answered, as if that explained it. He just nodded, and resumed talking to Lucas in hushed tones. "You guys know you don't have to whisper, right?" The two boys glanced at her.

"Sorry," Lucas said apologetically.

"No worries," she smiled.

Katie cut in, "More like Hakuna Matata." Regan laughed. The four girls used to sing the song at basketball practice for fun.

"What's that mean?" Lucas asked. Regan was surprised at first, but when she thought about it, it made sense that he didn't know what it was. She was fairly sure they didn't have TV there.

"It's from a movie called *The Lion King*. It's a classic on Earth, and 'Hakuna Matata' is a song in it. The saying means 'no worries,'" Rya explained. She was almost done cutting through the second vine, and Regan headed over to help her tie them around the dragons.

"Hey, Lucas, catch!" Rya shouted, tossing one end of the vine up to him. It was a long throw, but she was strong and it made it. Lucas caught it and tossed it down to Regan on the other side of Nakata. Taking the rope, she met Rya under the dragon.

"Lay it across your lap and hold it there!" she shouted up to him. He did so, and she pulled the vine tight and tied it to the other end. They finished quickly and hurried over to Ace and repeated the process.

"Alright, just let us get on the dragons and we can go," she told Emma, who was watching them.

"Good, I don't want to be riding back home in the dark."

"Yeah, sure. Hey, Nyx, let your wing down please?" she asked the black beast. Slowly, he lowered his right wing so she could clamber up to his back. She sat in front of Ace so she could see where they were going and tell Nyx where to go. Rya did the same on her dragon, placing herself in between Nakata's head and Lucas.

"Okay, where to?" Regan asked Ace. He pointed to a large mountain a little to the right of them. It was shrouded by a thick smoke, and reached high up into the sky.

"That's where your camp is? How do you breathe through all that smoke?" Katie asked incredulously, rejoining the conversation after talking to Emma. Ace shook his head.

"We live next to it. The volcano is dead. The smoke is from our many bonfires," he explained. While he was talking, Ember took off, the rest of them following.

"Why next to a volcano?" Emma asked. She was happier now that they were finally on their way.

Lucas answered this time, "Landmark. The hunters have to have something to know where the camp is when they go wandering to find food. Sometimes you end up really far away from camp."

"Makes sense." Katie replied.

"Why were you guys outcasts in the first place?" Rya asked suddenly.

"Rya!" Regan scolded. She figured the matter was probably a sore subject.

"It's okay," Ace replied. "We were sent out because we look different."

"What?" Katie sounded confused. Then, Regan remembered what Amanda's husband had said.

Lucas explained, "No red hair."

"They made you leave because you don't have red hair?!" Katie asked in complete disbelief.

"Yup. We don't have red or blond hair, so bye bye us," Ace joked, trying to lighten the mood.

"That's harsh," Emma remarked.

"No kidding." Regan thought about what would happen if Ann and Brian's rocket was successful. The amount of people who had red or blond hair on earth was limited, most people had brown.

Rya spoke up, her voice excited, "We're almost there!" Ace pointed to a clearing next to the volcano, surrounded by tall trees with grey bark and auburn leaves that threw shade over the large area. It was a little ways away from the camp, but close enough that it wouldn't take them long to walk the rest of the way.

"Land there," he said, "that way we won't scare them. The only dragons they've ever seen are the types that attack you." Regan nodded, and Nyx swooped in to land with a thud in the middle of the clearing, his claws stirring up a cloud of dust. Ember landed next to him, Angel and Nakata behind him.

"Let's go!" Rya shouted eagerly, rushing to get off Nakata. When Lucas tried to follow, his foot got stuck and he tripped. He crashed into Rya, who was still on her way down, and both of them landed in a heap at the green dragon's feet. Nakata snorted, a dragon's way of laughing.

"Ugh," Rya muttered. She shoved Lucas off of her and stood up, brushing dust and gravel off her shorts and shirt.

"Hey!" Lucas straightened up and glared at Ace, who was laughing heartily.

"Let's get going before anything else happens," Emma suggested, glancing at Rya.

"Yeah!" she replied, glaring at Lucas. He shrugged and headed for a gap between two trees.

"Just follow the path," Ace told them, and began following his friend. Regan could just barely make out a faded pathway that turned toward the camp. She gestured to her friends and began walking after the boys. Fairly soon, the six young kids arrived at the camp, where Lucas and Ace were greeted with a mixture of warmth and scolding.

"Where were you two? We've been looking all over for you!" an adult woman asked them angrily. She had the same color hair as Lucas and the same bright blue eyes.

Lucas began, "Mom-"

"I don't want to hear it. You two are in big- who are they?" Lucas's mom suddenly asked, her gaze shifting to the four girls. Katie waved awkwardly, and Rya smiled.
"I'm Rya, and this is Regan, Katie, and Emma," she introduced, gesturing to each of them accordingly.
"I'm Hannah," she smiled. "Boys, explain yourselves." her tone changed quickly from friendly to angry.
"Well, uh..." Ace trailed off. Just then, another woman came rushing up. She hugged Ace tightly.
"Never leave without telling me again, ok?" she told him.
"Okay, can you let go now. You're hurting my ribs."
"Oh, yes, sorry dear. Who are these lovely ladies?" she asked. Regan snorted at being called lovely, and Emma elbowed her in the stomach.
"We met them when we went to find food," Ace explained, once again introducing them. The lady smiled, and shook each of their hands.
"My name is Teresa. I am Ace's mother."
"Cool." Rya sounded like she didn't mean it, but Teresa didn't seem to notice.
"So what brings you here?"
"Well..." Now that they were actually there, Regan had no idea what to say.
Rya answered instead. "So you see, these mean people named Ann and Brian are planning to launch a giant rocket to Earth to invade and take their evil rules there and take over and they are almost done building it and we need your help to stop them. Will you help us?" The words came out in a jumbled mess, leaving Rya nearly out of breath.

Confused, Teresa and Hannah turned first to each other, and then to the rest of them.

"Is there somewhere we can go that's private?" Emma asked, noticing their confusion.

Lucas nodded, "Yeah, follow me. Come on, Mom." He motioned toward a small structure, almost like a *tipi*. It was quite large, made of large, reddish colored branches propped up against one another and tied at the top with something resembling a vine.

"This place is kinda cool," stated Rya as they walked toward the *tipi*. Looking around, Regan noticed there were many other buildings like the one they were headed toward, as well as a few made of large, square stones. People with black and brown hair milled about, with varying skin tones as well. She saw toddlers, elders, even young infants being carried by their parents.

"They kicked babies out too!?" Rya exclaimed, completely shocked. Ace nodded grimly.

"Those who didn't meet the requirements, yes. Some of them are the third child in their family. Their families got sent away before they were even born."

"That's so harsh!" Rya replied. Soon after the discussion, they reached the *tipi*. Lucas led the way in, the rest following close behind. Inside, the *tipi* was big and airy, the ceiling angling high above them. They sat in a circle around a circular stone table.

"So, tell me again why you are here." Hannah told them. Emma recounted what had brought them here, starting with their first visit to the Pride and ending with the journey to the camp.

"So, you want us to help you destroy a rocket Ann and Brian are building to take over your homeland?" Teresa asked when they were finished. They nodded.

"What's in it for us?" Hannah asked. Regan glanced at Rya, who shrugged and turned to the two grown-ups.

"Revenge?" She made it sound more like a question than a statement. For a second Regan wasn't sure if coming had been a great idea, but the two women turned to them and smiled.

"We're in," they said in unison.

"Yes!" Rya exclaimed.

"That doesn't mean that the rest of the camp is in too though. We'll have to take a vote at the gathering tonight," Ace's mom told them. Regan sagged a little. The chances of everyone agreeing were pretty low.

Rya, however, sounded fairly optimistic, "Okay!"

As they waited for the gathering to begin, the boys offered to show them around. They took them past the huge fireplaces where they ate, surrounded by dark, wooden logs for sitting on. Next they took the girls to their own hut, one of the few made of stone bricks. They shared the hut with each other and one other family of three. The six kids halted outside the door.

"How do you build these things?" Emma asked, her voice curious. Lucas shrugged.

"I have no clue. They were already here when we got kicked out. I have seen them being built though. It's kind of fun to watch."

"Can we go inside?" Rya jumped up and down in anticipation. Regan really couldn't see why she was so excited, but Rya could get excited over pretty much anything. The boys exchanged a glance.

"Sure, why not?" Ace said finally. He led the way inside, the others following close behind.

When they entered the hut, Regan was surprised to see the high, vaulted ceilings. From the outside it had looked fairly small. The space was divided into thirds, with giant beds occupying the beds to the right and left, as well as the wall directly across from them. They didn't look very comfortable, being made of wood with no mattress. Covering the beds were thin blankets.

In the middle of the room stood a small square table, made of the same red colored wood as the beds. Ace held up his arms.

"Welcome to our humble abode," he said wryly.

"Those beds look really uncomfortable," Rya said as she looked at them. Lucas shrugged.

"Eh, could be worse. At least we have the blankets. Most of the homes here don't even have beds."

Emma's eyes widened. "No beds? What do they sleep on?"

"The ground," Ace replied. "We were some of the lucky ones."

"Wow," was all Regan could say. She couldn't imagine having such living conditions.

"So, who leads the camp?" Rya asked. She went to sit down on one of the beds, placing her hands under her for more cushion.

"His name is Derrick," Ace told them. "He was one of the first thrown out this year."

"How long have they been doing this? Making you outcasts?" Regan asked. She wanted an idea of how many people were in the camp.

"Since the Pride was founded they've been throwing people out. Not many make it though, unless they find the camp." Lucas answered. Katie's eyes widened.

"How could someone be so heartless?" Regan asked. It was more to herself, but she said it out loud anyway. The boys shrugged.

"I don't know," replied Ace in a dejected tone. Rya's eyes brightened with anger.

"Why do you sound so hopeless? She hasn't got to Earth yet! This just proves why we need to stop her!"

Regan nodded. "Rya's right. It's not too late to stop this. They may have already killed many, but think of all the people we can save if we stop this now."

"True, it's definitely worth a shot," Ace acknowledged. Just then Teresa and Hannah walked in. The two mothers noted the grim looks on the teens' faces and glanced at each other.

"The gathering will be starting soon," Hannah told them, "Let's get going." She led the way out of the small home, starting toward the largest fire, in the center of the camp. Surrounded by large stones, similar to those the houses were built of out, it towered over them, casting a warm, red glow over them. Marveled by its beauty, Regan paused to stare at it. It was amazing to her that something so pretty could cause so much destruction when let loose.

"Regan, you coming?" Snapped out of her daze by Rya's voice, Regan nodded and continued following them. Once they got closer, she started to make out the shapes of people. Lots of them. Dancing in circles around the fire and singing happily, their voices floated to them on the air. Soon, she could feel the heat of the fire. She couldn't understand how the outcasts tolerated it. Even from there, where she was at least a yard or two away from the dancers, she was sweating, and it was becoming hard to breathe as well.

"How do they get so close to the fire without overheating?" she asked aloud. Lucas glanced back and answered with a smile.

"Fire planet, remember? They're used to constant heat from the volcanoes and lava pits."

"Right."

Sweating even harder now, she took a step back. "So when does that gathering start? They might not be hot, but I sure am."

Ace laughed, "It already has. The dancing is the opening ceremony."

Emma tilted her head. "Really? What's it for?"

Lucas shrugged, "I'm not really sure. Just kinda, tradition, I guess."

Regan nodded. "Makes sense." She glanced at Rya, whose eyes were reflecting the firelight, making them seem orange instead of blue.

"How long until Derrick comes? Won't we have to tell him our ideas?" Katie asked. It was a valid question. Then, Regan realized that they didn't have an actual battle plan. What would they tell them when they asked how they planned to accomplish their goal? Now she started to get nervous. Yet, as soon as she went to speak and tell them of the problem, out walked whom she assumed to be Derrick. Dressed in red flowing robes, he strode toward them. The leader of the camp had bright blue eyes and dark brown hair that was cut short. Throwing his arms out, he hugged Teresa and Hannah.

Her nerves grew. She wouldn't have enough time now to come up with a decent-sounding plan. They'd fail to convince the outcasts to help them, and the Pride would take their rocket down to Earth and destroy all of her friends and family.

Rya, sensing her nervousness, put a comforting hand on her shoulder. "It's gonna be fine," she said confidently. Regan forced a smile and glanced back to where the two moms and Derrick were talking quietly. How could things be okay?

She saw Hannah point to where they stood. Derrick nodded and turned to face them. All she could do was stand and watch while the three adults drew near them. Her knees were shaking and she shifted her weight from foot to foot, back and forth.

"Hello, ladies," Derrick smiled warmly. "I've heard that you have something to tell me?" Rya nodded.

"Yes, we do," answered Emma. She motioned for Regan to explain.

Slowly, she answered, "Well, you know Ann and Brian, right? And their terrible rules? Well, they're building a rocket now to take to Earth, where we are from, and are planning to implement their rules there as well. We came here to ask for your help in defeating them and making sure that rocket never makes it to Earth."

"So, will you help us?" Rya finished for her. The four girls looked expectantly at Derrick, waiting for his answer. Lucas and Ace watched him as well. Derrick turned to talk to Hannah and Teresa in hushed tones. When he faced them again, his expression was more serious than before.

"I cannot ask our people to fight alongside you without knowing they want to. If they are not willing, we will not help." he said, his voice full of regret. "I am truly sorry, but I cannot make their decision for them." Regan's heart plummeted. He went on, "The only thing I can do for you is give you the chance to ask them yourselves."

"When will we be able to do that?" Emma asked, sounding just as disappointed as Regan felt. When she glanced over, Regan could see that Rya and Katie looked down as well.

"As soon as opening ceremonies are done, you may ask," he answered. "I wish you good luck." He strode off, his robes swishing behind him as he went. Turning to her friends, Regan tried to put on a brave face.

"Hey, we still have a chance here. Remember how eager Lucas and Ace were to join in? And their moms?"

Katie replied, her voice cracking slightly, "Yeah, but there's no guarantee that's what everyone will be like."

"If we go in all sad and depressed they definitely won't be! How would you feel if someone tried to convince you to fight and they were acting like the fight was already lost?"

Rya shrugged. "Bad, I guess?"

Emma nodded, "I probably wouldn't join them."

Regan threw out her hands. "Exactly! All we need is to act confident and come up with a good battle plan before we get up there! After that, it's up to the people." The three girls nodded grimly.

"It's gonna have to be a pretty good plan," Rya admonished. Regan nodded.

"Lucas," she called, "how much time before opening ceremonies are over?"

He glanced toward where the people were still dancing. "Ten minutes, fifteen at the most."

She smiled. "Alright then, we have some work to do."

By the time the dancers began to slow, they had come up with a plan. A few of the camp members began to trickle away from the huge bonfire, gathering near the base of the volcano the camp was centered around. Gradually, the six young teens began to make their way to it as well. On the way, Regan reviewed the plan in her head. If she left even one detail out, it could ruin it.

Soon they were at the base of the volcano, surrounded by people with brown and black hair, blue eyes, darker skin. All of them were different, yet as equally crucial to the girls' cause as the next. Regan caught sight of Derrick moving near the front of the crowd, motioning for them to come forward. Pushing through the throng of people, they made it to where he was standing, at the base of a large outcropping of rock.

Leading up to the ridge was a staircase of stone, the same that made up the brick houses they'd seen. The boys wished them luck as the four girls followed Derrick to the top. Once there, Derrick introduced them to the crowd, his voice carrying easily over the distance.

"My people," he said, "we were all wronged when we were thrown out of the Pride." Regan heard murmurs of agreement being whispered. Derrick went on, "Even now they are still casting people away because of their looks. But these four girls may have a way to stop them, once and for all." Excitement grew amongst the people. Who were these girls? How could some kids defeat the villains that had been plaguing them their entire lives?

Derrick turned to them, his blue eyes glinting in the dim light. "You're up."

Her mouth dry, Regan stepped up to the front of the rock, Rya not far behind. Looking out over the people, she saw thousands of eyes, all trained on her. Against the dark rock of the volcano, the four girls seemed tiny, formidable leaders being a thought that never crossed the minds of any watching them. But, in spite of her fear, Regan spoke, her voice ringing loudly so everyone could hear.

"We just recently met the Pride and their leaders, Ann and Brian. At first they seemed friendly, but as we kept meeting up with them, they grew more and more suspicious. We finally learned of their rules yesterday, and found out that they are planning to fly a rocket down to Earth. They mean to implement their rules there as well. As of now, over half of our Earth's population would be likely to die as an outcast. That's around four billion people." Gasps of horror rang out among the mass.

This time Rya joined in, "We ask for your help in defeating the Pride and its leaders."

A young man's voice rose up in a question. "What's your plan to beat these guys?" The girls had been expecting the question, and Emma answered it readily.

"Since the Pride trusts us, we'll enter as 'friends.'" She added air quotes to emphasize the word. "After we are in, we'll go to their office where we have a camera set up. You'll be on the other end of the camera, watching."

Katie continued, "Eventually, we'll give you a signal for you to sneak in and get as many people out as you can. We don't want to harm anyone who isn't doing something wrong. Some people were just lucky enough not to get thrown out." Regan could see people nodding their heads. Emboldened by this, she went on with the explanation.

"After you get everyone out, you'll say a code word that we will have decided on. We'll be able to hear you with special pills we'll take before we go in." More nods followed.

"Once we hear the code word, two of us will slip out to help you with the rocket. The other two will tie up Ann and Brian," Rya told them. Grunts of confusion followed the part with the two leaders. Rya emphasized, "We plan on saving those two for you." Nasty grins broke out on many of the men and women's faces. Rya grinned as well.

Regan finished the explanation. "Then, we'll break into the room where the rocket is stored and destroy it." She smiled, confident that most of the people would go with it. A few questions did, however, need to be answered.

"How will we know which room the rocket is in? I lived there, and I never saw even the slightest sign of a rocket being built!" a young woman called out. Regan nodded.

"The camera in the office has audio. Once we get it out of Ann and Brian, you'll be able to hear it and can go from there."

"What about the guards?" asked another one. "How will we take them out?"

Regan and Rya glanced at each other, and turned back to answer in unison, "Dragons."

Fear began to stir in the people, along with worry. *Dragons? How would they control a dragon? What if it ate them? Dragons weren't tame, they were wild animals, waiting to swallow you in a single gulp.*

Their fears were quelled by Regan's next words. "I know you're all thinking we're crazy, but I promise you, we aren't. We found a nest of four dragons not long after we arrived here on this planet. They were very friendly, and gradually, we tamed them. Now we can ride them. They'll be the ones helping us with the guards."

Words of excitement and awe floated around the crowd. Tame dragons? No one had ever heard of such a thing.

Then, the question she'd been dreading was asked. "How do we know we can trust you?" shouted an older man. He had a walking stick, and his hair was straight white. Regan panicked. She had no idea how to make them trust them.

Seeing Regan's expression, Rya stepped up. "Your hunters were sick, weren't they? Maybe it's something we've seen on Earth. If we can cure them, will you trust us?" Nods and shouts of yes were heard. Derrick walked back to the front of the rock.

"Are there any more questions?" he asked. No one spoke. "Very well. I will introduce these four girls to our sick hunters, and if they cure them, we will meet again here to vote on this plan of theirs. This gathering is over." he finished, turning back to the girls with a swoosh of his robes. He was barely visible against the red rock of the mountain, and it being dark made it even harder to see him.

"That went well," Katie remarked as they were led back down the mountain. Regan nodded.

"Yeah, good thinking on the hunters, Rya. That was brilliant!"

Rya blushed, "Aw, thanks."

"How are we going to fix the hunters though? What if it isn't something we've seen before?" Emma inquired. Regan shrugged.

"Guess we'll just have to wait and see."

Katie jumped in, "Where are we going to sleep tonight? We can't just stay here, can we?"

Derrick answered her with a smile, "You are welcome to stay. You can also come back tomorrow if you wish to sleep in your own beds."

"I vote own beds," Rya said enthusiastically. Regan laughed.

"Well, I guess we'll be back tomorrow then. Let's say goodbye to the boys before we leave though." Her friends agreed, and left Derrick to go find them. They spotted them sitting next to the slowly dying bonfire with a few other young boys. As soon as they saw the girls, they jumped up and ran over to them.

"That was awesome!" Ace exclaimed, smiling broadly.

"Yeah! How did you guys come up with such an awesome battle plan?" Lucas asked, his voice a pitch higher than normal. Regan laughed.

"I don't know. Teamwork?"

"Can we go? I'm tired," Rya whined.

"She is yawning a lot," Emma conceded.

"We can leave now, I guess," Regan said, waving to the boys. "Bye guys!" They waved back.

"See ya!" Lucas yelled. The four girls walked back to where the dragons were. When they got there, all four huge beasts were wrestling with each other. Legs were tangled everywhere and heads bit playfully at others tails.

"Pfft, wild beasts. Sure," Regan laughed, remembering both what the two Pride leaders had said as well as what the people told them. After seeing this, how could anyone think these magnificent animals couldn't be tame?

"Alright, break it up," Rya told the dragons loudly. Slowly, the dragons untangled themselves, Ember snorting a plume of fire as he stood up. Once they were up, the four dragons stood in a line, like soldiers in the army, and put up their wings in a salute. Regan could've sworn Nyx was smiling.

"Aw man, look what Lucas taught them!" Emma exclaimed. Regan laughed.

"Aren't you smart?" she asked the big animal, stroking his nose affectionately. He snorted, nuzzling her. Laughing, she got on his back, running up his wing as usual. By this point, Katie no longer needed help getting on Angel. The small girl waited patiently for her friends to mount.

After they were on, she asked, "Can we go fast?" Regan glanced at her, an eyebrow raised.

"Aren't you scared of falling off?"

"Yeah," Katie admitted, "but I also don't want to be seen by the Pride either." Regan tilted her head to one side. Katie had a good point. Then she got an idea.

"Maybe we don't have to go fast to avoid being seen." Leaning down the Nyx's head, she asked, "Can you use your power to disguise us somehow?" Turning his large golden eyes toward her, he gave a slight nod. Surprised at the almost human movement, Regan watched as a fog of darkness covered them. Trusting that the dragons could see through the cloud, she took off, Nyx's wings beating silently as he glided through the air. The other three dragons were just as quiet. Flying through the air, she looked up, where the dark from his power wasn't covering, and gazed at the stars. She smiled, knowing these were the same stars her parents, sisters, and friends were seeing back down on Earth.

The ride home was quiet, all four girls deep in their own thoughts. Once they touched down in front of their home, the darkness dissipated. Regan slid down Nyx's wing, landing on the ground with a soft thud. The others did the same.

"We should get some sleep before tomorrow," Regan said. "The whole plan rides on us being able to cure those hunters." Her friends nodded.

"I'll set out the medical kit so we can just eat and leave in the morning," Emma told them, heading for the kitchen. The other three were close behind, but instead of staying in the kitchen, continued on to the bedroom. Settling comfortably under her blankets, Regan said goodnight and went to sleep.

Chapter 7

The following morning was full of excitement. They ate a quick breakfast of bacon and the potato-like plants. When they were finished, they hurried to clean their plates and be out the door. Sensing the emotions of the girls, the dragons were outside pacing and roaring happily. Grabbing the medical kit, Regan led her friends out the door. Swiftly, they mounted the dragons and were on their way, Emma holding the medical equipment tightly, having had it handed to her by Regan before they mounted. Regan trusted her pale friend to hold on to it more than she trusted herself.

The flight back to the camp went by in a blur. Now that the dragons knew the way, they were more confident and the going was quicker. Landing in the same spot they had the day before, the four girls rushed to get off their dragons and make it to the camp. Nervous and excited as they were, they tripped over their own feet and fell quite a few times on the way. However, they just laughed off the mishaps and kept going, keeping the same sprinting pace.

As a consequence, when they finally reached the camp, all four friends were struggling to breathe, their sides heaving with the effort.

"Well, look at us," Regan laughed, "rushing into things, as always."

"This time, literally rushing," Rya puffed. Laughing, their voices wheezy, they walked to where they saw Derrick waiting for them, near where the huge bonfire had been the night before.

"Hi, Derrick," Katie panted, smiling. The walk had given them a little time to catch their breath, but all four still had gut aches from the run. Noticing the state of them, the camp leader smiled as well.

"Welcome back, ladies," he said warmly. He led them toward the largest of the stone houses. It was twice the size of the other houses, almost as big as the girls' own dome.

"This is our hospital," he told them. "You'll find the sick hunters in there."

"Do you know if the sickness is contagious?" Katie asked. Derrick shook his head.

"As of now, we don't know much. Most have been coughing and sneezing a lot. Some of the worst ones are having chills and fevers. I've heard some even complaining of their muscles aching." he told them.

"We'll try our best to help them." Katie told him confidently. He nodded and left them. Rya led the way, entering the building through its large, square-cut door. Her friends weren't far behind.

Inside the huge building, beds, just like the ones they'd seen in Ace and Lucas's house, were lined up against the walls. The smell of sickness greeted them as they walked amongst the hunters. Some had thrown their thin blankets off, while others were buried under piles of them.

"Those symptoms he told us, don't they sound kind of familiar?" Katie asked. Emma nodded.

"Yeah, but a bunch of different illnesses have the same symptoms. It's really just the combination of effects, what causes the sickness, and how to treat it that are different," she told her small friend. Kneeling down next to one of the hunters, Emma put her hand to his forehead, her pale skin contrasting sharply against his dark brown.

"He definitely has a fever," she announced.

"Wait a minute!" Rya said, her voice high-pitched. "Coughing, sneezing, fever. It's the flu! They all have the flu!" She was right, Regan realized.

"You're right!" Katie exclaimed.

"Does anyone remember how to treat the flu?" Regan asked. Emma nodded.

"We just drank a bunch of water and rested. I think there are some pills you can take to help with the symptoms, but I'm pretty sure they wouldn't be in here." She answered, holding up the medical bag. Regan nodded.

"Let's ask how much water they've been giving them and go from there," she suggested.

"Yeah," Rya agreed. The two of them walked back outside, Emma and Katie staying to see what they could do for the sick men and women. They headed toward a small woman with short, black hair and brown eyes standing near the entrance to the hospital.

"Hey, do you work with the sick people in the hospital?" Rya asked. The woman nodded.

"Sorry, my name is Regan, and this is Rya. We're here with our friends Emma and Katie to cure the sick hunters." Regan told her. The woman straightened, her brown eyes brighter.

"Hey, you were the four who were speaking yesterday at the gathering!"

Regan nodded, smiling. "Yeah, that's right."

"I'm Diana," the woman told them.

Rya interjected, "We were wondering if you could answer a question for us."

Diana nodded quickly, "Fire away."

Regan was the one to ask the question. "How much water have you been giving the sick hunters each day?" Diana took a moment to think.

"A cup or two each day. It's the same ration everyone gets, since there's not a stream close by."

So they're all dehydrated, she thought to herself.

"Ok, thank you for your time," Rya thanked the lady. Diana nodded, grateful to be of service.

"It was a delight."

Turning away from the dark haired Diana, they walked back to the bed where Emma and Katie were still kneeling. Emma was rummaging through the medical bag looking for something. Katie noticed the two girls coming back and tapped her friend on the shoulder. Emma too looked up from what she was doing, hurrying to stand up when she saw who it was.

"Did you find anything out?" she asked when they were close enough to talk. Rya nodded.

"Yeah, we met this woman named Diana. She was really pretty. Black hair and blue eyes. She was really nice too. She-"

Before she could continue rambling, Regan interrupted her, "She told us they only give them one or two cups of water a day. Apparently they don't have a stream very close by." Rya glared at her friend for the interruption, but said nothing.

"Wow, no wonder they haven't recovered yet." Emma said with shock.

"We have the stream back home, can't we bring them water from there?" Katie asked.

Shaking her head, Regan replied, "No, it's too far. Most of the water would splash out of the bucket before we get back here."

"So, we'll have to find a closer stream?" Rya finished, making it sound like more of a question than a statement. Emma nodded.

"It's either that or bring them all with us back home. And with as many as there are," she gestured to the many people lying on beds, "it makes more sense for us to just bring the water to them."

"Makes sense," Regan agreed. "Want us to go scouting for a closer river while you stay here and keep an eye on them?"

"Yeah, me and Katie can stay. You and Rya go. If the boys are brave enough they can go too. We have two extra dragons," Emma pointed out.

"Good point. We'll go find them and then we'll leave. As soon as we find something we'll come back and get you so you can see it for yourselves." Regan told them. The four friends said their brief goodbyes, and then the two friends were on their way again. Finding Lucas and Ace sitting inside the boys' house talking, the girls filled them in on the plan.

"Sounds good to me!" said Ace, thrilled. He would get to ride one of the dragons! A real, live dragon! Lucas's response was equally as excited.

"Let's go!" the dark haired boy yelled, pumping his fist. The two girls laughed and led the way back to the clearing where the dragons were. This time, instead of wrestling, the four beasts were napping. Nyx had his little sleeping mask made of dark clouds covering his eyes again. Slowly, Regan shook him awake, making sure not to startle or scare him in the process. They might have been tame, but a scared dragon was not a good thing, even if that dragon was friendly.

"Which one do I get to ride?" Ace asked, looking hopefully at Nyx. By now all four dragons were awake, roaring and yawning loudly. Regan shook her head, laughed, and pointed to Ember and Angel.

"I call the red one!" shouted Lucas, despite knowing Ace was bigger. Clumsily, Lucas tried to mount the drake. After sliding off the beast's back multiple times, he finally managed to stay put. Grabbing onto Ember's crown of horns, he laughed and waved back down at a scowling Ace. The big boy looked dubiously at Angel, her small delicate wings folded neatly against her sides.

"Will the little one be able to carry me?" he asked.

"Yeah. She's small, but she's still really strong too. You'll be fine," Regan reassured him. Still wary, Ace climbed on Angel's back. After seeing no sign of weakness or struggle from the white dragon, he relaxed.

"Alright, everyone ready?" Regan called.

"Yep," Rya shouted back, giving a thumbs up. Regan smiled, and Nyx took off. With a whoosh of air all four dragons were off the ground and flying high into the air.

"Remember, we're looking for streams and rivers. This isn't a joyride," Regan reminded upon seeing Lucas with his arms flung wide and his tongue sticking out. Embarrassed, he quickly composed himself and acted like nothing happened.

Fairly soon, Rya pointed out what looked to be a small river. It ran horizontally from them, and very nearly fit the description of a stream. However, there was enough water there to help the hunters recover, and it was only a mile or two away from the camp. With the dragons, they could easily transport the water.

"Let's land and get a closer look. We need to make sure it's safe to drink," Regan said.

"Alright," Rya replied. Nakata landed first, her feet sending up clouds of rust-colored dust. Nyx wasn't far behind.

Rya was off her dragon first, sliding gracefully along Nakata's wing towards the ground. Regan did the same. Lucas and Ace, their rides being smaller, decided to jump off the dragons' backs. Ace landed somewhat gracefully, bending his knees to soften the fall. Lucas, however, hit the ground and tumbled, causing more dust to spray. Regan and Rya both stifled laughs. He stood up slowly, brushing off his clothes. Turning to glare at them, he walked toward the river.

"How do you know if it's safe to drink?" he asked. Regan walked over and knelt next to him, sticking her hand in the water as she did so.

"Normally, the faster the water is running, the better. All rivers are freshwater so we don't have to worry about that." Feeling that the current was pretty strong, she then looked up and examined the ground around it, as well as the rock-covered bottom of the river. "Another thing to look for is animal activity. If the animals are drinking from it, it's safe."

"There are some tracks over here!" Rya shouted from downstream. Regan went to join her, and sure enough, there were animal tracks. They resembled hooves, and covered the ground around them.

"Good eyes, Rya," Regan praised. Rya beamed.

"Thanks." Turning back to the boys, who had followed Regan over, she gestured to the water source.

"I'd say it's all good to drink," she told them.

"How are we going to transport the water?" Lucas asked. She hadn't thought of it, but it was a valid question.

"We should be able to find a container with a lid on it, right? We can use those to carry the water without having it spill everywhere." Rya answered.

"Good idea. Do you have anything like that at the camp?" Regan asked. The boys glanced at each other, then nodded.

"We should be able to find something like that," Ace replied. "They won't be completely watertight, but they'll work."

"Good enough," Regan responded. "We might have some containers in some of the extra domes too."

"We good to go then?" Rya inquired.

"Should be. You boys ready?" She tilted her head towards them, and got a quick nod in reply.

"Yep, let's go," Lucas said, running to make sure he got to ride Ember again. Ace sighed and walked back to Angel.

"Angel is not *that* bad," Rya admonished. Ace shrugged.

"Yeah, she isn't. But who doesn't want to ride a fire dragon? Like, he literally breathes fire!" He threw his arms out in the flame drake's direction. Ember had shot a plume of fire into the sky, snorting happily when he did so. Regan assumed it was the dragon's way of showing off.

"He has a point," Regan said to Rya, who nodded thoughtfully.

"True."

"Alright, let's leave before Lucas and Ace get into an argument over Ember," Regan laughed.

Rya smiled, "Alright."

"I'm right here you know," Ace interjected, causing Regan to chuckle. By now they had reached the dragons, and everyone mounted smoothly. They took off, flying effortlessly back to camp. They talked on the way back, mostly about what Earth was like. Both Lucas and Ace were very curious people, asking many questions about what animals were there and what the girls' home life had been like. The four kids grew much closer on that short ride.

Fairly soon, they arrived back at camp. They landed in the now familiar clearing. They walked back to the hospital, where they found Emma and Katie talking to a few of the hunters. They had to have woken up while they'd been gone, for all of the hunters had been asleep when they left.

"Did you find any water?" Katie asked as they walked in. Nodding, they told them of the small river and of Rya's idea to use sealed containers to carry the water back.

"Sounds like a good plan to me," Emma said. She was holding a cool cloth to a female hunter's forehead, trying to break the girl's fever.

"We should start looking for the containers now. Lucas and Ace, you two can stay here and look. Rya and I will fly back to the domes and look there."

"Ok, just hurry. The sooner we get these hunters healed, the better. The longer we wait for the attack, the longer Ann and Brian have to finish that rocket," Emma warned.

"Alright, we'll go fast," Rya replied. The two girls ran out of the building to reach their dragons. The boys rushed out too, but headed in a different direction to start looking around camp. Rya and Regan took all four dragons, thinking to tie any container they couldn't carry to Ember and Angel's backs. They got on the dragons and were on their way, flying speedily back to the domes. They didn't talk much on the way, the wind from flying so fast making it hard to see, let alone speak.

Once they reached the domes, they landed and dismounted in front of the girls' dome, the dragons flying over to their nest, which was right across from their living quarters. Regan pointed to the left of their home.

"I'll take right, you take left?" she stated it as a question.

"Okay," Rya confirmed. They each ran to the decided upon sides. Regan threw open doors and slammed them close as she went. She made sure to check every cabinet and storage space as she went. There was a new sense of urgency in the air, now that they'd been reminded of the importance of their mission. If they arrived even seconds after the rocket was launched, they'd be too late. Not even a dragon could beat the speed of a rocket.

By the end of the search, Regan came up with ten gallon sized containers made of thin, see-through plastic. The containers reminded her of the milk jugs they had at home, on Earth. Rya's loot was similar, yet she managed to find fifteen. Quickly, they determined that each girl could carry three of the containers without falling off their dragons. The rest they tied to Angel and Ember's backs with vine ropes made by Nakata. They made sure the jugs were secure before taking off again. They reached the camp with little mishap. After landing, they left the containers next to the dragons and went to see how many the boys had found.

It was the boys who found them first. Lucas sprinted toward them, his hands full of woven bowls that seemed to be sealed with something similar to clay on the inside. A few fell as he ran toward them, but were picked back up by Ace. The bigger boy's hands were also overflowing, and it was nothing short of a miracle how he had picked the dropped ones up without dropping any more.

"How many did you find?" Rya asked, breathlessly.

"20 in total," Ace answered, his sides heaving.

"How much water can they hold?" Regan inquired.

Shrugging, Lucas replied, "I'm not sure. We'll find out soon enough." They tied the containers they couldn't carry to Nyx and Nakata's sides. They also tied each individual lid onto their containers. Then, they mounted and were on their way.

Once they got there, they got off and untied the lidded containers. Surprisingly, nothing had fallen off. When they dipped the bowls and jugs into the water, the cool clear liquid flooded them, filling them with the precious substance. They talked easily with each other as they worked.

It took them quite a while to fill all the bowls they had brought with them, and by the time they finished they were sweating from the heat. Their chatter had quickly died as they grew more and more tired. The sun was almost down. Quickly, they finished filling the bowls. The boys and Rya were in charge of completing the task, while Regan worked to tie the lids back on to the ones they were done with. She tugged on each vine, making sure the lids were secure. Carefully, she set the heavy containers over near the dragons. She began to wonder if the dragons were strong enough to hold all the water plus their passengers. She shrugged off the idea. Surely they could do it, right?

After they were done filling and tying every last one of the containers, they attempted to tie them back on the dragons. Two of the teens would hold up the water-filled jugs, normally Ace and Regan as they were the strongest, while the other two tied them on with the same pieces of vine Nakata had produced earlier for the same purpose. The work was hard, Regan and Ace having to heave the water jugs up to shoulder height to be able to tie them on correctly. Lucas and Rya had many different scrapes and cuts from the rough vines.

Finally, they were finished. Every one of the jars, jugs, and bowls had been filled with water and tied onto the dragons. Slowly, the four friends climbed back on their dragons and set off. They didn't talk much on the way back. All of them were sore from lugging around the heavy, liquid-filled containers. Regan struggled to keep her eyes awake on the ride.

The ride back went fast, however, and soon they approached their usual landing spot. Dismounting with groans of pain, the four teens each untied two jugs of water. Together, they carried the water back to the hospital. When they trudged through the large opening, each of them carrying two gallons of the precious liquid, Emma and Katie turned to greet them. It was kind of hard to make out the two figures in the dim light.

"Woah, that's a lot of water!" Katie gasped. Regan closed her eyes and nodded.

"Yeah," she sighed. "There's a lot more we still have to carry in." Lucas and Ace cautiously put down their water, making sure that none of the water spilled. Rya and Regan did the same.

"Well, we can take a break from this and help you guys," Emma offered. Rya shook her head vigorously, despite how tired she was.

"Oh, yes please!"

Emma laughed, "How many did you fill?"

"Forty-five," Lucas answered. The two girls' eyes widened.

"Better get to work now then," Emma noted. Lucas led the way back out of the hospital, but was quickly overtaken by Katie and Emma, whose legs weren't as sore. By the time the two girls reached the dragons, the boys, Rya, and Regan were well behind. Katie and Emma waited for them, impatience making them anxious.

"Hurry up!" Emma called.

"Please?" added Katie, ever polite. The four kids quickened their pace. Eventually, they reached their friends.

"Next time, don't wait," Rya told her friend. "We'll go faster if we don't stop." Emma nodded.

Ace undid one of the vines, letting loose fourteen of the jugs. Each person grabbed two water-filled containers, but there were still two left.

"I'll take one." Katie offered. She'd noticed earlier how tired her friends looked. She glared pointedly at Emma, knowing her friend wouldn't think to offer on her own. Emma saw the stare and raised an eyebrow, then seemed to understand.

"I'll take the other one," she said. Rya nodded gratefully.

"Thanks," said Ace, thankful not to have to lug another one around when he was already sore and weary. Emma smiled and picked it up. Together, the three jugs she was carrying were heavy. Regan was more worried about Katie, however, because she knew Emma was strong. Katie was much smaller and still had to carry the same amount of weight. They began walking back to the hospital, going even slower than they had when they'd come. Regan could see Katie ahead struggling to carry the third container, juggling the three around in her hands to avoid dropping them. The others were oblivious to Katie's efforts, partly because of the setting sun. She took bigger steps to catch up with her small friend.

She caught up to her friend just as Katie finally dropped the container. Regan leaned down and caught it in one hand, holding her two bowls tightly against her body with her other hand. Katie smiled.

"Thanks, Regan," she told her.

Regan nodded, "I can carry it now. If that's okay with you?" She added the question because she didn't want to hurt her friend's feelings. By now the others had noticed, and slowed to watch the exchange.

"Yeah, that is fine. You're stronger than me anyway," Katie admitted with a laugh. Regan grinned.

"Bravo! Bravo!" Rya shouted. All six friends laughed together. With the mood uplifted, they quickened their pace. They arrived back at the hospital joking and laughing with each other once again. The pressing matter of Ann and Brian's rocket had been momentarily forgotten.

"Emma and Katie staying here again?" Rya questioned. Regan could tell she wanted a break.

"Why don't we get the camp members to help?" Lucas interjected. Regan wondered why she hadn't thought of it before.

"That's a great idea!" she exclaimed. "You and Ace want to go get some volunteers? We need a few to stay here and distribute the water." Ace and Lucas both nodded quickly and left. As soon as they were out the door, Rya sat down with a sigh.

"What a day," she said. Emma nodded.

"What a week," Katie added with a grim laugh. Now that she thought about it, they hadn't really been on Vulcan that long. With everything that had happened, it seemed like months had passed, rather than just a few days.

"No kidding," Regan replied. "First we tame dragons, then we find actual, living people."

"Then we find out those people are evil and trying to destroy our home planet. And now we have to stop them," Rya finished with another sigh. She laid down on the ground, stretching out her aching muscles. She laughed, "Can't get much better than this, huh, guys?" For once, Rya sounded the opposite of optimistic.

Katie tried to pick up the slack. "Everything will be fine. We'll heal the hunters and stop Ann and Brian. Right, Regan?" Her three friends turned to her. She didn't know what to say. She didn't know if the water would help. She didn't know if their plan would work. She had no idea what lay ahead of them, but she knew she had to put on a brave face for her friends.

"Right," she said. Katie brightened. Just then Lucas and Ace walked back in, leading a group of ten or more young boys and girls.

"These are our friends, Rya, Emma, Regan, and Katie," Ace introduced, pointing to each of the girls as he said their name. Regan waved when his finger landed on her. A few of the kids gave a smile in return.

"You know the plan. Who wants to stay and give out the water?" Lucas asked. A few hands shot up. "Alright. Gigi, Henry, and Ruby are going to stay here and help the hunters. The rest of us are going to help carry the water over here. Got it?" The kids nodded. "Alright, ready, Regan?"

"Yep," she replied. She marveled at how Lucas took leadership. The boy she had come to know was a far cry from who she was seeing now. This version of Lucas was more confident, more responsible.

"Okay, let's go." Lucas motioned to Regan, "Lead the way." She smiled, and started out the door. Rya, Katie, and Emma weren't far behind. The new kids followed the girls, Lucas and Ace bringing up the rear. They kept a quick pace walking back to the dragons.

They reached the clearing, and when the dragons came into sight Regan heard gasps of fear. She turned to look at a panicked Lucas.

"May have forgotten to mention that part," he said nervously. She twisted back to look at the frightened boys and girls.

"It's alright, guys," she said reassuringly. "Watch." She walked up to the dragons, who were sleeping peacefully. Again, she heard shrieks of fear from the kids. She headed for Nyx, the giant animal curled into a ball, his huge tail curled over his snout. She sat next to Nyx's neck and ran her hand along his warm, scaled neck. She glanced back at the boys' camp friends, and saw a mixture of surprise, awe, and fright on each of their faces.

"See everything is fine. I'm gonna wake him up now," she told them. Cautiously, a few nodded. Whispering to the dragon, she said,

"Time to wake up, Nyx." The great dragon woke, the golden pools of his eyes turning to look at her. She smiled at him as he nudged her hand. He wanted to be petted. She rubbed his neck for him, and he in turn twisted his neck to encircle her in a sort of hug. She heard faint cries of surprise, muffled by the dragon's thick hide. Nyx must've heard the noise as well, for he broke the hug and turned to look at the kids.

"See? Nyx is friendly. So are the other dragons," Regan told them, prompting her friends who had previously been watching to head over to their dragons. Her friends gradually woke up their own dragons as well. Regan saw a hand rise up out of the small group of kids.

"Yes?" she called. A small boy who looked to be a few years younger than her stepped out, his black hair messy.

"Can we pet them too?" he asked in a high voice. Smiling, she nodded.

"Come up here with me. Don't run too fast though. We don't want them to get scared. They don't know you yet," she explained. The little boy shook his head in agreement, and slowly made his way to her and Nyx. The dragon stood up to greet the new person, towering over everyone gathered there. The boy didn't stop, however, and continued walking up to them. When he reached Regan, she noticed his knees were shaking.

"Here, hold out your hand so he can sniff you," she said to him. Slowly, he held out his hand. Nyx leaned down his head and sniffed it, blowing out huge gusts of air with each breath. Satisfied that the boy was friendly, Nyx head butted the boy in a gesture of kindness, but which sent the boy sprawling. He rolled on the ground and came to a stop a few feet away, lying on the red dirt face first. Concerned, Nyx flew over and started sniffing and licking the boy. The boy rolled over laughing. Regan smiled at the success. Gradually, they got everyone to trust the dragons.

When they were all okay with being around the dragons, Ace tried to start to untie the containers. By now it was almost pitch black out, and the big boy could barely see where his hands were. After struggling with the rough vines for a while, he gave up and turned to the girls.

"I can't see my hands, much less where the vines are. How are we going to get the containers off the dragons now?" he asked.

"Can't we just wait till morning?" Rya suggested.

Regan shook her head. "If we wait, the dragons could accidentally squish the containers and all the water would come out. We have to at least get them off and away from the dragons before we go to bed."

Emma brightened, "Ember has a fire power, right? Can't we start a fire and do it that way?" Regan grinned.

"Good idea, Em! Let's get some branches from these trees and make a bonfire." They gathered the young boys and girls who were still playing with the dragons and told them Emma's idea. The kids were excited to help, and began picking up branches and piling them near the dragons. It took a while because it was dark, but it was worth the time. When they were done, they had a pile of sticks that was three or four feet tall.

"Ember!" Emma called. The drake trotted over, flaming embers blowing out of his nose when he breathed. "Set it on fire, would ya?" The dragon gave what seemed to be a nod, but was hard to see in the darkness. Then, they saw a bright plume of flame spit out of the dragon's open mouth, lighting the stack of dry tinder on fire. A bright blaze went up from the branches, causing a reddish-orange glow to light up the area around them. It was more than enough for them to see, and Ace started again to undo the knots securing the water-filled jugs to the sides of the dragons. This time he was helped by Lucas, as well as Regan and her friends. It didn't take long for the six friends to untie all of the containers, and they soon had them all scattered around on the ground.

"Alright, everyone grab a container! Take two if you can!" Lucas ordered. Obedient, the kids all took a container, the older and bigger kids grabbing two. Together, they managed to grab all twenty-three of the containers that were left. They gathered together where the trail started, the fire still blazing behind them.

"Angel, put that fire out please," Katie asked her dragon. A stream of white frost shot out from her mouth, chilling the air around them. It smothered the bright fire, blanketing the twigs that served as tinder as well. The fire was out, and in its place was a pile of frost covered branches. Satisfied, Katie turned back to her friends.

"Come on, guys, let's get back to the hospital so I can get some sleep," Rya said loudly. She made her way to the front of the group, barely visible in the now complete darkness. "Follow me!"

They followed Rya the whole way back. Occasionally someone would trip on an unseen stone or stick, but those around them would help to pick them back up, as well as the jugs they dropped. Regan was proud of the teamwork shown by her friends and the volunteers. With

Rya leading the group, her voice calling back every now and then with encouraging words, they made it to the camp. They stopped in front of the hospital.

"Okay, everyone, let's get the water inside the building. Then we can all get to bed," Ace told them. Murmurs of agreement went around the group. Regan went in first, dropping her jugs near the back of the room. The others followed.

"Just hand me your jugs, and I'll set them down for you," she whispered. She didn't want to wake up the sleeping hunters. Everyone tried to hand her their containers at once.

"One at a time people," Rya put in.

"Form a line," suggested Ace. Obediently, the volunteers formed a line behind Lucas.

"Need help?" he asked Regan as he handed her his jugs. She shook her head, then remembered that he probably couldn't see it given how dark it was.

"No, it's fine. It'll go smoother with just one person."

"Ok, I'm gonna go then," he told her.

"See you tomorrow!" she whispered loudly.

"See you," came the reply. Then another bowl of water was shoved into her hands.

"Hey, what would you like us to do?" said a voice behind her. Regan jumped.

"Sorry, did I scare you?"

"Possibly," Regan admitted to the voice. She put down the bowl and accepted another. "Who would you be?"

"Gigi. One of the three who stayed to help the hunters?" Now Regan remembered. "Ruby and Henry are here too."

"Um, would you like to help move water? I can hand it to you and you can find an open place to put it." She had just sent away Lucas when he asked to help, but since the three had nothing to do they might as well help. Besides, the floor around her was starting to get crowded, and since she was sitting she started having to reach behind her to place each container down.

"Yeah, we can help with that," Gigi moved behind the jars and jugs that Regan was leaning against. "Come on, guys." Two people who must've been Ruby and Henry shoved their way next to Gigi.

"Ready?" Regan inquired.

"Yeah," said a voice that sounded higher than Gigi's. Regan guessed it was Ruby.

"Okay then, here you go." Regan handed back a milk jug full of water. It was taken from her by strong hands, and she could hear it being placed down. They continued the train of handing and placing until every one of the containers had been set down.

"Good work, guys," Regan praised. The only people still left were the three who had been helping her, Ace, and her friends.

"Thanks," answered Ruby. The three made their way to where Ace and Rya were standing, talking in hushed tones. "So what now?" Regan shrugged.

"Go home and get some sleep," Rya answered.

"Sounds good to me," answered Henry, his voice deeper than the other two volunteers. The four girls said their goodbyes and left, leaving Ace and the three helpers to get home on their own. They walked blindly back to the dragons, struggling to see in the darkness.

Eventually, however, they found the dragons sound asleep in the middle of the clearing. They woke them up gently, making sure not to scare them. Nyx and Nakata both roared softly, a dragon's form of a yawn, and stretched. Climbing onto his back with a groan, Regan made sure her friends were mounted as well, and then took off. None of them talked much on the ride back home. They were all tired and sore from working all day.

When they got to the domes, they landed in front of their home. After the girls dismounted, the dragons headed toward their nest to finish out the night. Emma led the way to their dome, yawning as she walked through the front door. The other three weren't far behind. They took off their shoes near the entrance and made their way to the bedroom. Neglecting to say their goodnights, they all fell straight asleep.

Chapter 8

The next morning, Regan woke up to an empty room. She stretched her arms and legs, threw off the covers, and went to the kitchen, where she found Katie and Emma making breakfast. Rya was sitting in the living room, talking loudly about their old basketball team.

"Do you remember that time when... Oh, hey, Regan!" she said happily. Regan smiled.

"Good morning," Regan replied, "What were you guys talking about?"

"Basketball," Katie answered. The sizzle of the bacon stuff could be heard, and Regan's mouth watered. Rya's stomach growled.

"When is that going to be ready?" Regan's best friend asked. "I'm starving!"

"Me, too," Regan admitted. Emma waved a spatula at her.

"It'll be done soon."

"The bacon is ready now," Katie added, holding out a plate piled with large strips of the salty food. Regan walked over and grabbed a piece.

"Be careful, it's still..."

Regan took a bite and flinched.

"Hot," Katie finished. Regan tilted her head. Her mouth was on fire. Emma watched, amused.

"Yep, definitely still hot," she told Katie, her eyes squinted. "Dang."

"I tried to tell you," Katie said innocently.

"You did," Regan acknowledged. She set the piece of bacon down on the table. "I'll let that cool now."

"Glad it was you and not me," Rya laughed, earning a glare from Regan.

"Food's ready!" Emma called before Regan could reply. Rya jumped up. Emma set down a big bowl of hash browns and a plate of the sausage-like meat.

"Is it cooled down enough?" she asked, cautious after Regan's incident. Emma nodded.

"Should be."

"Why doesn't Regan taste test it first?" Katie joked.

"No way. Rya, do it," Regan replied quickly.

"Why do we even need to taste test it? I said it was fine," Emma asked.

"Good question," Regan turned to look at Katie.

"I mean, if you say it's okay," Rya took a spoonful of the hash browns and plopped them onto her plate. Sitting down at the table, she took a small bite of the food.

"These are good!" she exclaimed. Regan sat down next to her and took one of the sausages. She bit into it, tasting the salty meat.

"These are, too!" Together, they enjoyed the meal. They joked and talked about school, sleepovers, and basketball games. They didn't mention Ann and Brian, however, or the rocket, and they barely even talked about the camp. Regan didn't want to talk about that stuff. It was so serious, and she needed a break from all the stress and worry it caused. Her friends were the same way.

After they finished their breakfast, they got changed and went to see the dragons before they took off for the camp again. Nyx was just waking up, but the other three were flying in circles over the nest, roaring and grunting happily. Ember nipped at Nakata's haunches, the big green dragon turning to snap right back at him. Angel joined in on the fun, flying over to bat at Ember's snout with her clawed foot. Regan smiled. It was nice to have such a playful and joyous morning when so many things were rough. Rya whistled up toward the dragons, calling for their attention.

Nakata heard it first, swinging her giant head around to glance at her owner and friend. Nakata swooped down to greet them. Angel followed, leaving Ember confused in the sky. It didn't take long for the flame drake to figure it out too, though, and he soon joined the two female dragons at the girls' sides.

"Nyx, you up?" Regan asked loudly. She entered through the huge, square-cut doorway to find him stretching, his mouth open in a wide yawn. He stopped mid-yawn and stared at her. Regan laughed. "You lazy!"

Nyx closed his mouth haughtily. Regan shook her head. "I'm just teasing. I know you're tired." She stroked his head affectionately, Nyx leaning his massive head into the caress.

"So when are we leaving?" asked Emma. She, Katie, and Rya had entered the dome while Regan had been joking around with Nyx. Regan shrugged.

"Up to you guys."

Rya answered, "Why don't we go now? There's nothing keeping us here, and the sooner those hunters are healed the better."

Regan hesitated. She didn't want to leave the dome, with the air of happiness still around them, to leave for a hospital full of sick, coughing hunters whose health was their only chance of getting the campers to trust them. She was tired of having to fight, having to prove herself. But, it was their only shot at saving Earth. Rya was right.

"Yeah, makes sense," Regan told her friends. "Let's get going then."

The four girls each mounted their dragons, none of them in need of assistance after having done it so many times. Regan smoothly ran up Nyx's wing to jump on his back. He was so large that in the past her legs had hurt because they were so far apart. She was used to it now though, and settled onto his back with ease. She gripped his horns tightly, preparing for takeoff.

"Everyone ready?" she called.

"Yes!" came the reply. In unison, all four dragons lifted off the ground, their great wings causing dust clouds to form. The dust swirled under them as they flew up and out of the dome, soaring away from the dragons' nest and the girls' home.

The ride to the camp was full of tricks and jokes. Angel twirled in the air a couple times, making Katie laugh with glee. Nyx performed a somersault in midair. His wings had to stop flapping to do so, resulting in them plummeting down to the ground. Regan screamed with fear, as well as with awe and laughter. They didn't fall far before Nyx completed his trick and started to beat his wings again.

"Show off," Regan muttered. Nyx snorted at her. She could've sworn he was laughing at her.

"That was awesome!" Rya yelled. She leaned down to her dragon's ear. "Can you do something like that?" Nakata did what seemed to be something like a nod, and dove suddenly toward the ground. Rya, in similar fashion to Regan, screamed in delight. Just before they hit the ground, the great green dragon pulled up short, her wings moving quickly to force them up again. Rya laughed. "That was amazing!"

Ember watched as his friends did their tricks, then looked hopefully up at Emma. Emma glared down at him, shook her head, and crossed her arms. She balanced precariously on his back.

"No way," she said firmly. Still, the red dragon's golden eyes peered up at her, begging her to let him. Again, she shook her head.

"C'mon Em! Let Ember have some fun!" Regan encouraged her friend.

"Yeah, don't be a scaredy cat!" Rya added.

Indignant, Emma retorted, "I'm not a scaredy cat!"

Katie shook her head, catching on to Regan and Rya's plan, "Oh, yes you are!"

"I am not!" Emma said again, this time the annoyance showing clearly in her voice.

"Prove it then," Regan challenged. Emma looked at her dragon, his eyes still begging with her, and gave in.

"Oh, fine! Just once though." As soon as the words were out of her mouth Ember dove, flipping around in a circular motion. Regan couldn't tell if her pale friend was laughing or crying when they finished the flip. Emma answered the question for her.

"That. Was. Awesome!" her friend yelled, giving a fist pump to emphasize her words. Regan laughed.

"Told you!" Rya shouted. By now they were approaching the camp. They swooped around the mountain and touched down in the clearing. By now there were paw and claw marks scattered all across the red dirt. There were also wide, shallow dips in the ground where the dragons slept.

After landing, Regan slid down Nyx's wing, landing neatly on her feet. She checked to make sure her friends landed safely as well. Emma stumbled once, but regained her footing quickly. Other than Emma's little mishap, their landing went well.

"Do you think they already gave the water out?" Katie asked as they strode toward the camp.

Regan shrugged, "Maybe."

"Lucas and Ace could've done it," Rya pointed out.

"Or Gigi, Ruby, and Henry," added Emma. They both had good points.

"I guess we'll just have to wait and see," said Regan. They continued along the trail until they reached the camp. They headed for the hospital, visible by its roof, which stood high above any of the normal houses. The four girls weaved through the stone homes, there being no straight path to the hospital.

They reached the hospital rather quickly. Upon entering, they found Lucas and Ace just beginning to give out the water in small, clay cups.

"How much water have you given out?" Rya asked. Regan walked over to where they had piled the jars and containers the day before. Only a few were empty. Ace and Lucas shared a glance.

"Around three or four?" Ace estimated. Katie raised her eyebrows.

"We just started!" Lucas exclaimed, quick to defend himself and his friend.

Regan laughed, "Guys it's fine. That just means we have a little more work to do."

Rya groaned, "Really? More work?"

"Do you want to save earth or not?"

"Well, yeah..." she trailed off.

"Then get to work," Regan finished. With a sigh, her best friend joined her by the jugs.

"Where are the cups?" Regan asked Lucas. He gestured over near the entrance, where a stack of the clay cups was sitting on a rough wooden table.

"I'll get them," Emma offered. Regan nodded, and the pale girl went to grab them. Katie hurried to help her.

"How long do you think it'll take for us to distribute all of it?" Katie asked. Unlike Rya, Katie wasn't whining. It was a question born out of curiosity.

"We've been here for half an hour, and we only have four done," Ace put in. He handed his last filled cup to a shaggy-haired hunter, who took it gratefully, then returned to talking to the blond-haired woman next to him. Most of the hunters were engaged in conversations with the people in their neighboring beds. Ace walked back to Regan and Rya and waited for the extra cups.

"So probably all day," Emma finished for him. She had just gotten over with the cups, and handed a small stack to Rya, who started slowly filling them. Regan took Katie's larger stack. Quickly, she filled up three and handed them to Ace. He nodded. Taking one in each hand, he sandwiched the third between them, and carried the three cups over to where he left off. Lucas too came over and grabbed two cups. Emma and Katie began helping carry the water as well. Soon they had an efficient system going.

"This is working pretty well," Rya remarked. They'd been working for an hour, and already had another twelve emptied.

"Yeah, the extra hands are really helping," Lucas said, taking yet another two cups from Regan.

"At this rate we'll be done by noon," said Emma.

"Yeah, not bad," replied Katie.

"So what happens after we give out all the water?" asked Ace. He handed a cup that was filled to the brim with water to an older hunter with graying hair. The man's arm trembled as he took the cup, spilling it onto the floor. Ace took the cup back and helped the man drink it.

"I don't know," Regan answered. "I guess we hope for the hunters to be healed and go from there. Basically the whole plan rides on us being able to help these guys." Ace nodded, and took the now empty cup back to be refilled.

It was around noon when they finished emptying the containers and jugs. They restacked the cups on the front table and separated the girls' bowls from the ones the boys had borrowed from the camp members.

"We can help you return them," Rya offered. Lucas shook his head.

"It's ok, I think you guys should talk to Derrick about the hunters."

"Why?" asked Emma.

"He can keep an eye on the hunters while you're at home," explained Ace, catching on to his friend's thought train. Regan nodded.

"Makes sense. Do you know where we can find him?"

Ace shrugged, "Probably in his hut near that stone outcropping. You know, the one where you gave your speech?" He pointed to the ridge at the base of the mountain. Sure enough, there was a stone building around 25 yards away from it.

"Alright, we'll head there then. Sure you don't need help?" Regan asked to make sure.

Lucas nodded and smiled."Yeah, we'll be fine."

"Okay then. Let's go, guys," Regan led the way to the red house, walking along a wide, well-worn trail that curved like a snake toward the stone building. Most likely it was formed by the people who walked to the stone outcropping for meetings. Once they reached the rock formation, the trail swerved toward the house. Trees and bushes were scattered around the path. This part of the trail was fainter. Soon, they reached the small house. Rya made her way to the front of the group and banged on the door loudly.

"Rya!" Regan admonished.

"What?" replied her friend. Just then Derrick opened the door.

"Well, hello, ladies," he greeted warmly. "Please, come in."

With a smug smile directed towards Regan, Rya entered the home. The other three girls weren't far behind. Inside the house it was bright, the many windows letting in lots of light. It smelled a little like smoke. Regan assumed it was because of the nearby volcano. The house was made of red stone bricks, same as the other buildings.

"So what brings you here?" Derrick asked. He was dressed in a pair of well-worn jeans and a faded black long sleeved shirt. It was very simple compared to the flowing red robes he'd worn when they first met. He sat down in a brown leather chair, gesturing across from him to a wide couch. It was only built for three people, so Rya elected to sit on the ground.

"We wanted to talk about the hunters," Katie told him, settling into the seat.

"We've identified that they have the flu, but there isn't much more we can do than to give them a bunch of water and hope they get better," explained Emma.

Derrick nodded slowly, "I see. How long do you think it will take for them to heal? As of now we are surviving on the plants the elders and children find."

"Hopefully soon," Rya replied.

"Okay, thank you for your help. I will call you back or have those two boys get you. Lucas and Ace, correct?" Derrick asked.

Regan nodded. "Okay, that sounds good."

Derrick stood up. "Now, I must be going. I have a baby shower to attend to."

The three girls on the couch stood up as well, Regan lending Rya a hand to help her get up. Rya took it gratefully.

"Oh, okay. We'll be going now then," Emma said, her voice clearly showing her surprise at the shortness of the meeting. Regan glanced at her, but said nothing.

"Thank you again for helping us," Derrick said as he ushered them out the door.

"Your welcome?" Rya replied. She barely got the words out before the door was slammed in her face.

"That was weird," stated Katie.

"No kidding," Regan said in reply. She turned back toward the camp.

"I guess we're leaving then," said Emma. Regan nodded, and started walking back to the hospital, where their containers and milk jugs were waiting. As she went through the camp, she noticed the little kids running around laughing, and their parents watching them with amused expressions. It made her miss her parents and sisters back home.

Once they reached the hospital they started picking up the now empty jugs. They had seen no sign of Lucas or Ace. They waited a little while to say goodbye, but eventually gave up and went to find the dragons. They tried to divide the twenty five containers up equally, but Regan ended up having to carry a seven instead of six like her friends. On the way to the dragons, they each dropped containers multiple times. Someone would drop one, then bend down to pick it up and more would end up falling.

Eventually, however, they reached the clearing. The dragons were sitting there, waiting attentively for the girls' arrival.

"They must've heard us coming," Regan said, dropping her containers into a very disorganized pile. Her friends did the same.

"Now we tie them back on?" Emma asked.

Rya nodded, "Yep. Every single one."

Katie groaned, "More work?"

Regan hit her lightly on the back, "Hey, stop complaining. We have the rest of the day to rest once we get these back home and put them away."

Katie tilted her head to one side, "Fine."

With the help of Nakata, the girls once more tied the plastic containers to the dragons' sides. The vines they used were rough, but by now they were used to the chafing they caused. This time they didn't divide the jugs up equally, but did it by the dragon's size. Angel, being the smallest, had four, and Ember had six. Nakata carried seven, while they tied the last eight to Nyx. None of the dragons took any notice of the containers. The plastic jugs were light, and the girls had tied them in a way that they wouldn't disturb the dragons' wings when they flew.

"Okay, let's go," said Regan when they were finished. All four girls mounted their dragons and took off, a cloud of dust forming below them.

On the ride home they discussed the topics of Derrick's weirdness at the meeting and the hunters' health.

"I didn't know they had baby showers here," said Rya. Nakata's wings blocked Regan's view of Rya's face when the green dragon flapped, but Regan could hear the disbelief in her friend's voice.

"Me either," Emma replied. They almost had to shout to be able to hear each other in the rush of wind. It seemed that the dragons were just as excited to get home as the girls.

"Yeah, it did seem kinda weird," Regan agreed.

"I hope the hunters get better," said Katie.

"Yeah, me, too," said Rya.

"What happens if they aren't healed?" Katie asked her in a worried voice.

"I don't know," Regan replied. "I guess we'll find out." After that the girls were silent.

They arrived home and immediately began untying the containers from the dragons. This would be the last time they had to untie them. Quickly, after having had so much practice, Regan and Rya undid the many knots securing the plastic jugs. The jugs, along with the vines, dropped to the ground. There they were picked up by Katie and Emma. The two girls separated the vines from the jugs, putting them into piles. It didn't take long for the girls to get all of them sorted out.

"Are we going to take the jugs back to where we got them from or just put them in our dome?" Rya asked as she picked up a few of the containers.

Regan shrugged. "Whatever you want to do is fine," she replied.

"Why don't we bring them to our dome?" said Emma. "Then they're already there if we need them later."

"Good point," Regan acknowledged. She headed for the building. Rya quickened her pace to catch up. Emma and Katie ended up being farther behind as they still had to stoop down and grab some. Regan and Rya reached their home a few minutes before their friends, and they took the time to decide where to put the jugs. Twenty-five plastic containers were a lot, and they had to figure out where they had enough room.

"Hey, wasn't there an empty room in the back?" Rya asked.

"Wasn't it the other one in that hallway? The one where the bathroom is?" Regan answered.

Rya nodded, her blond ponytail swinging, "Yeah, that one! How 'bout we take these in there? It can be a storage room or something."

"Ok," Regan replied. Rya led the way.

A few seconds after they left the kitchen, Regan heard the door open.

"Back here!" she called. Soon, Katie and Emma joined them.

"Where are we putting these?" Emma asked. Both girls' arms were piled high with containers. Katie could barely see over her stack. Regan motioned with her head to the empty room.

"In there. Remember, there was a room with no stuff in it? We only went in there on the first day we came."

"Oh yeah! Good idea!" praised Katie.

Rya's smile was smug, her blue eyes shining brightly, "I came up with it," she said proudly as she walked into the room.

Regan laughed, "She did," she said. She followed her friend into the empty room. Rya was currently dumping her containers in the back left corner of the room. As the house was a dome, the back hall was curved a bit. It was how it was with all the rooms in the house. Regan walked over and added her jugs to Rya's. Emma and Katie did the same. The pile was now up to Regan's knee, the jugs precariously balanced on one another. It didn't matter much though. It wasn't like they had anything else to put in the room.

"How many were left?" Regan asked as they walked out of the room. The concrete floors scraped against her tennis shoes as she went.

"Only a few," Emma replied. "I can go back out and get them if you guys want to start on lunch." The past few days, when they had been working with Ace and Lucas, the girls had eaten at the camp. The dragons had continued to hunt for them, and the girls and their new friends had feasted on the animals the dragons had brought for them. They had used the fireplaces to cook them, and everything extra they had given to the citizens to eat. Everyone had been really grateful for the food.

"Ok," Regan agreed. Emma left to go grab the other containers and the other three girls walked back to the kitchen.

"What should we make?" Rya asked. Regan shrugged.

"How about pork? There was another one of those huge pigs outside," Katie suggested. Regan shook her head vigorously.

"Please no. We've had too much pig recently," she said.

"Ok, then what about steak?" Katie tried.

"That sounds yummy," said Rya.

"Steak is fine," Regan concluded.

"I'll go grab it," Katie told them. She walked out the front door to the kill pile as they now called it. Regan had seen a huge bull lying at the base of the pile earlier, and she assumed that was what Katie was going for. It made sense, as they didn't want something that big going bad.

Regan wondered why the dragons kept killing things instead of eating what they'd already killed. She figured it was probably because the creatures overestimated how much the girls could eat. She imagined the dragons would think the girls' diets were similar to their own, resulting in them bringing in multiple giant animals for them to eat, when in reality they only needed a small fraction of what they were hunting.

"Okay, you get the pan out, I'll wash up some fruit," Regan said to Rya. Rya nodded, and moved to grab a pan out from the cupboards. Regan went to the fridge. Even though it was a really ugly yellow-brown color, and it smelled terrible, the fridge still did what it was meant for. She opened the door, plugging her nose at the stench, and pulled out a blue bowl with a navy lid. She opened it and found that it was full of blueberries. The dragons had found a patch of them nearby and Regan's friends must've gone and picked some while she was still sleeping. As there wasn't a sink in the kitchen or bathroom, Regan walked outside to the stream that wound like a snake through the domes.

Stooping down, she opened the lid slightly to let the water in. Then she dipped the whole bowl into the stream, making sure none of the berries fell out. After the bowl filled with water, she took it out of the stream, and closed the lid just enough so that none of the blueberries would fall out. Then Regan tipped the bowl over in her hands so all the water drained out. When she was done, the blueberries were all clean.

She walked back into the dome to find Katie and Rya cooking the beef on the stove. The smell of it made her mouth water.

"Is Emma back yet?" Regan asked, setting the bowl of blueberries down on the table, which had already been set.

Just then Emma walked out of the hallway, "What'd you say?"

"She asked where you were," Katie informed her before Regan could answer.

"Well, I'm here," Emma said to Regan. Regan laughed.

"Yeah, I can see that."

Emma moved toward the stove. "So what did you guys decide to make?"

"Steak," Rya said. She flipped the large piece of meat to reveal the other side, which was cooked perfectly. The smell wafted toward her.

"That smells really good," Emma said. "Anything I can help with?"

"No, not really," Katie replied. "Regan washed the blueberries, and we're cooking the meat."

"Fine with me," Emma sunk into one of the wooden chairs surrounding the giant dinner table. The legs creaked under the weight. The pale girl stretched out her arms, and for a second Regan thought she was getting ready for a nap. Regan plopped down next to her with a sigh.

"Meat's ready!" Rya called out after a couple of minutes. Katie then came over, holding the meat with a pair of tongs, and dropped it onto the biggest plate the girls had.

"Now that is what you call a steak," Regan laughed. Rya grabbed a knife and started cutting it up. She gave the largest piece to herself.

"Jeez, Rya," said Emma.

"What?" Rya asked. "I'm hungry!"

Regan laughed, "Can't tell." After everyone had a decent-sized portion of meat on their plate, as well as a handful of blueberries, they began eating. The meat was salty and the blueberries were very sweet. Regan thought it was one of the best meals she'd had so far on the planet. She cleaned her plate in a matter of seconds. So did Rya. Regan took both of the finished plates and started washing them. Rya dried them after they were clean. Emma and Katie handed their plates to Regan, too. Pretty soon all of the dishes had been washed. Emma put away the bowl of blueberries. Katie left to throw the leftover bones to the dragons. Regan could hear the sounds of growling and roaring as the four magnificent beasts fought over the tiny bones.

"What now?" asked Rya when everything was cleaned and put away.

Regan shrugged, "I guess we wait until we go back to the camp tomorrow," she said.

"That's fine with me," said Emma, who immediately headed over to the couch. She fell on it with a sigh, and almost instantly fell asleep. Her pale skin was bright against the greenish brown leather of the couch.

"You know, a nap doesn't sound too bad," Rya said. Instead of going to the couch, Rya went into the bedroom to sleep. Regan went with Katie to go hang out with the dragons. They were still fighting over the last of the bones when the two girls walked out. Upon seeing Regan, Nyx stopped fighting and trotted over. He followed the girls until they finally sat down with their backs against the outside of the dragons' dome. He curled up around Regan, his tail lying limp. The huge triangle-like spike on the tip of his tail lay harmless between the two girls. Regan ran her hand along the dragon's side, barely able to reach it as he was so large. His stomach was turned toward her, the scales darker there for camouflage. Nyx purred loudly, his golden eyes shut in contentment.

Angel, who had just then noticed the girls' presence, walked over as well. Her white scales gleamed in the gradually fading light. The spike on the end of her tail reminded Regan of the head of a spear. Other than her tail, nothing about Angel seemed vicious. Her eyes seemed to Regan soft and kind, and even the Angel's teeth looked nice compared to the other three dragons. The dragonet settled down on the other side of Katie.

"When do you think NASA will figure out that transportation system they said they were working on?" Katie asked Regan.

Still stroking Nyx's side, Regan shrugged, "No clue, but hopefully soon. I can't wait to see my family again," Regan told her.

Katie nodded in agreement, "Yeah."

They talked for a little while, then fell asleep. When Regan woke up, it was very dark outside. Katie was still sleeping, as were the four dragons. Sometime while they'd been napping Ember and Nakata must've joined them because Ember was curled up next to Angel and Nakata was on the other side of Nyx. Picking her way through the pile of claws and tails, Regan reached Katie and bent down to pick her up.

"Probably not good for you to sleep out here," she said quietly to herself. Katie wasn't very heavy, being as small as she was, and Regan easily picked her up and carried her to the house. Once she made it to the bedroom, Regan carefully laid Katie down in her bed. After she was sure Katie was fine, she headed for her own bed. She could hear Rya's faint snoring when she climbed under the covers. It didn't take long for her to fall asleep.

When Regan woke up again it was morning. She slid out of bed and threw her blond hair into her customary ponytail, then began walking towards the kitchen. When she walked past the other beds, she noticed that everyone was still asleep.

When she made it to the kitchen, she pulled out the leftover blueberries and rewashed them. Then she set the table with plates, spoons, and napkins. She also filled up four cups of water. After that she placed the big bowl of blueberries in the center.

"That's not going to be enough food," she muttered. She went outside to where the kill pile would be, but all she found were bones. A scavenger must've eaten the rest of the decaying animals at the bottom. The dragons were gone too, probably to hunt for more food.

Disappointed, she went back inside. By now Emma and Rya were up, and both girls were standing at the table looking confused.

"How come there's only blueberries?" Rya asked.

"It was all we had, and the dragons' kill pile is just bones now." Regan answered. "Sorry."

"Well, can't we just ask the dragons to go hunt?" Emma suggested. Regan shook her head.

"They're gone. Probably hunting right now."

"Why don't we just wait then?" Emma said. Just then, Rya's stomach growled loudly.

"That's why," Rya told her. The three of them sat down and began their meager meal. Eventually, Katie joined them, her hair a ratted mess. She didn't question why it was so small, just sat down and started eating. She looked exhausted.

"Are you okay?" Emma asked her, the girl's blue eyes searching Katie's worriedly.

"I'm fine, just tired. I want this all to be over with," Katie answered, yawning as she did so.

"You can stay here while we go check on the hunters," Regan told her.

"I'll stay with you," offered Emma. Katie nodded slowly.

"As long as you two promise to hurry and get back here to tell us what's going on," she said to Regan and Rya, emphasizing the statement by pointing with her spoon. "I don't want to be stuck here worrying all day."

Rya nodded, "Yes, ma'am."

"We'll get back as soon as we can," Regan added. Quickly, the two friends finished their meals, said their goodbyes, and were out the door. They found the dragons chewing happily on a giant pig. The kill pile, however, had not grown at all, but was still a sad pile of gnawed bones. Nakata saw them first, and growled playfully at Rya.

"Nakata, get over here. We're leaving," Rya called to the big green beast. Obedient, Nakata trotted over. Nyx followed her.

"Good boy," Regan said, glad she didn't have to yell at him like Rya had. Gracefully, the two friends mounted and left. As they flew, Regan's eyes watered. The wind kept whipping her in the face, and she was grateful that she'd tied it back earlier. Rya wasn't having such luck. Her short blond hair couldn't fit in a ponytail, and was blowing into her eyes and mouth constantly.

"Having fun over there?" Regan laughed, earning a glare from Rya. Finally, she caught sight of the volcano that marked where the camp was. Swiftly the dragons flew to their normal landing point and touched down. Regan slid down the wing Nyx put down for her. Nakata did the same for Rya.

"Thanks, guys," Regan said to the dragons. Nyx snorted in response. Together, the two girls rushed toward the hospital. They didn't want to waste any time. Upon entering the building, they found the beds empty. Regan and Rya shared a glance.

"Is this good or bad?" Rya asked.

"Hopefully good," said Regan in reply. They walked back out and saw Ace talking to a few of the kids who had helped carry the containers.

"Ace!" shouted Rya, waving her hand to try and catch his attention. It worked, and Ace ran toward them, a huge grin on his face.

"It worked! The hunters are healed! We're holding a meeting tonight to vote on helping you or not!" he said happily.

"That's awesome!" said Regan.

"Yeah! But where's Lucas?" Rya asked.

"He's with his mom, I think," Ace told them. "Where's Emma and Katie?"

"Katie was feeling tired, so we let her stay home, and Emma said she'd stay with her," Regan said. He nodded. They'd have to go get them before the meeting started.

"We'll have to go back and get them now, won't we?" said Rya, voicing Regan's thoughts aloud.

"Yeah."

"I can't believe it worked," Ace put in. "I'm pretty sure a lot of people are going to vote in favor of fighting with you guys too."

"Sweet!" said Regan. "What time is the meeting?"

"This afternoon. They wanted to have it earlier in case they wanted to fight. That way they have more time to prepare for the battle," he explained.

Regan nodded, "Makes sense. We should probably go get Emma and Katie soon then."

"I can go get them by myself if you want to stay here," Rya offered.

Regan hesitated, "Are you sure?"

Rya nodded with a smile. "What are you worried I'll get lost? I'll be fine. It's not like I can get hurt either. I have Nakata."

"True," Regan acknowledged. "If you're sure you want to, I'm okay with staying here."

"I'm sure. You go find Lucas and try to convince people to fight with us," Rya told her. Regan nodded, and Rya left toward the dragons.

"Take Nyx with you!" Regan called after her. "I don't want him here alone." Without turning, Rya gave a thumbs up.

Regan turned back to Ace, "Let's go find Lucas."

He spun to face the house he and Lucas had shown them a few days before.

"He should be in the house," he said to her. "If not we'll have to look around." She followed him to the building and looked inside. Sure enough, there was Lucas. He was sitting on one of the very uncomfortable-looking beds talking to his mom. She turned to greet them with a smile.

"Regan, right?" Hannah asked, pointing to her. She smiled.

"Yep."

"Weren't there three other girls with you the last time we met?" Lucas's mom asked.

"Yeah, two are back at home and the other is going to get them before the meeting starts," Regan informed her. Hannah's eyes lit up.

"That's right! I totally forgot about the meeting! Congratulations, by the way. I am so grateful that you young ladies could heal my husband."

Ace interrupted before she could say anything else, "Could we borrow Lucas?"

Hannah smiled. "Yes, of course. I should've known you were here for him. Silly me. Go along, honey." The last part was directed at Lucas. He stood up quickly and joined them at the door.

"Bye, Mom!" he called over his shoulder as they walked out. "So, what do you guys think will happen at the meeting?"

"I think that we'll get to fight," Ace answered, his voice hopeful.

"Me, too," Lucas replied. "Anyone hungry?"

"Starving," Regan told him with a laugh. He pointed to a pig on a spit above one of the many fires. It wasn't nearly as big as the ones the dragons caught, but it was still pretty large. Juice dropped into the fire below it.

"That looks really good," Ace remarked.

"Are you sure we can eat it?" Regan asked. In response, Lucas, his dark hair blowing wildly in the wind, went over and sawed a piece off with a knife he'd found sitting nearby. He took a giant bite of the meat, juice dripping everywhere.

"That is good! And yeah, it's fine. This one was caught by my dad."

"Is your dad a good hunter?"

"The best!" said Ace. Lucas handed him a piece of the pig. "He killed this all by himself! Didn't he, Lucas?"

"That's right! Shot it clean through the heart with his bow," Lucas replied, the pride clear in his voice.

"Dang." Just then, Rya, Emma, and Katie spotted them. They ran to join them.

"Woah!" said Rya upon seeing the meat. "Now that looks good."

Lucas nodded. "Yeah, it is." He handed each of the girls a small portion of the animal.

"Be careful," Ace warned them, "It's probably still hot." Rya, however in her hunger, disregarded the warning and dug in.

"Yep," she choked out, her eyes watering, "Still hot." Katie blew on hers before eating.

"I think it's fine," she said after taking a bite. Rya glared at her.

"So are you feeling better, Katie?" Regan asked her friend. Katie nodded.

"Yeah, I was just tired."

"So when's the meeting starting?" Emma asked them.

Ace answered, "This afternoon. We can go explore the volcano while we wait if you want. There's lots of cool lizards and things."

"Yeah, that sounds fun," Regan replied.

"Maybe we'll see a Ryzard!" Rya said excitedly. Regan laughed.

Everyone's stomachs were full by the time they finished their meal. Once they had cleaned all the juice off their fingers, they left for the volcano. Ace and Lucas led the way around it, pointing out and naming all different kinds of animals. Regan caught sight of one of the stubby-tailed raccoons she had seen on their first few days on the planet. They did end up seeing a Ryzard as well, which Ace told them was properly called a spiked-back lizard.

"Is not," Rya replied when Ace told them what it was. "It's a Ryzard." Regan just shook her head and laughed. Rya was stubborn as a donkey sometimes.

They finished exploring the volcano around noon and walked back to the camp. The adventure had gone by in a blur because they were so excited about the voting. By the time they got back, it was time for the meeting.

"I'm so nervous!" Katie confessed as they followed the crowd of people. The group was carried toward the rock outcropping that had held the last meeting, at which the girls had told the camp about their plan.

"Same here," Emma agreed. She almost had to shout to be heard above the chatter produced by the mass of people. Anxiously, they waited for the meeting to begin.

Finally, they saw Derrick on top of the platform.

"Welcome, my people," he started. "Today is to be a historical day. This afternoon, we are to decide whether we will stand by these four girls," he gestured to where they were standing, "and fight against the Pride, or if we won't go into battle with them." Murmurs sprang up around the crowd.

"Now," he continued, "before we vote, Hannah would like to say a few words."

"Your mom is talking?" Ace asked, surprised.

"I guess so," Lucas looked just as shocked as Ace. Then, Hannah's strong voice interrupted them.

"Hello," she said. Regan thought she sounded shaky. "Many of you might know my husband, Shawn. I don't know about any of you, but he was very grateful to be cured after that illness swept through." A few of the people around them nodded.

"I've just started to get to know these girls, but my son, Lucas, is already very good friends with them. They've already helped us heal our sick hunters, shared their food with us, and most of our children are even friends with them."

More nodding. "What reason don't we have to stand by them and help them in this fight? We can even rescue the friends we left behind from these monsters that call themselves leaders." She paused. "Take that into consideration when you cast your vote. I know what my vote will be." With that, she left the rock.

Applause broke out among the people. Regan clapped as well. She figured citizens didn't normally go up and give a speech that good.

"That was amazing!" Rya exclaimed.

"Yeah," Lucas said proudly. Gradually, the applause ended.

Derrick once again took his place at the top of the outcropping.

"Seeing as Hannah has said her part, we will now vote." He paused and looked around at the crowd. "Remember, this is a big decision. Don't make the wrong choice."

"What's he mean by that?" Emma turned to ask them.

Regan shrugged, "No clue."

"All in favor, raise your right hand, and say 'I.'" A flood of hands rose above them, and a chorus of 'I's rumbled like thunder. The six friends turned to one another and smiled.

However, they missed Derrick's agitated frown.

"All against, raise your left hand, and say 'Nay.'" Regan heard someone say it, but when she stood on her tiptoes and looked around, she counted only ten hands that were up.

"Oh my gosh, we did it!" Katie screeched happily. The people around them glanced at the girls, smiles plastered across their faces.

"Well done, ladies." said an older man. "You've convinced us."

"I can't believe it!" Emma added.

"Me either," Regan admitted, slightly embarrassed by her own lack of faith. Excited talk about the upcoming battle surrounded them.

Regan barely made out the shape of Derrick leaving the rock, his red robes swishing behind him.

"Let's go celebrate!" said Lucas. He grabbed Regan's wrist, who in turn held onto Rya, and dragged her out to the edge of the crowd. Rya must've grabbed Katie and Emma too, because when they emerged from the mass of people they formed a giant chain, Lucas at the front, Emma on the end. Ace came out a little after them looking dizzy.

"Everybody's going crazy," he told them. "They're so excited to finally get revenge on Ann and Brian."

"I would be, too," said Emma with a shiver. Just then, Hannah popped up behind them.

"Congratulations, girls!" she said breathlessly, her eyes shining. She wrapped them up in a hug.

"Thank you!" Regan replied after she let go. "Without you, many of those people probably would've voted against us!" Hannah shook her head.

"Don't thank me. It was the least I could do after you healed Shawn."

Rya smiled. "Well, thank you all the same. Now, who's up for a party?"

Chapter 9

The celebration lasted well into the night. People danced around the bonfires and sang loudly. They prayed for help in the upcoming battle. They shared stories of hunting expeditions and ate the trophies of those hunts. Pigs, smaller than the one Lucas's father had shot, were served, along with many bison-like animals. It was the best night yet for Regan on Vulcan.

She and her friends hung out with Lucas and Ace for most of the party. The boys introduced them to many of the young children of the camp. They played lots of games with the small children, and by the time the celebration was over, Regan was exhausted. But the night had been so much fun, she didn't want it to end.

"See you guys tomorrow," she told Lucas and Ace when they left for their dragons.

"See you!" Ace shouted after them. They made it almost to the edge of the trees that bordered the clearing when Derrick stepped in front of them. However, Rya, who was leading, didn't see him in the pitch dark. She had almost run into him when they heard his voice.

"Well done, girls."

Rya leapt back in surprise, accidentally knocking down Regan, who was right behind her.

"Jeez, Rya," Regan said, annoyed.

"I apologize," Derrick said blankly. "I must've scared you."

"Wow, I had no idea," Regan muttered under her breath. She glanced around to make sure the others were okay before hauling herself up.

"It's ok," Katie said hurriedly, apparently guessing Regan's annoyance.

"Would you like us to come back tomorrow to go over the battle plans?" Emma asked him. After she said this, Regan began to wonder why Derrick had approached them now. Why hadn't he said anything at the party, when there was still daylight?

"Yes, that would be helpful." He sounded interested, but at the same time Regan felt he was angry at them. For what, she didn't know.

"Okay then," Katie said, "we'll see you tomorrow morning then." Without another word, Derrick turned and left them.

"Huh," Rya remarked. "That was weird."

"You know, it kind of reminds me of when we went to his hut that one day," Emma told them. "Remember how he said he had a baby shower to go to?"

"Yeah, he's been acting strange lately," Rya agreed.

"Maybe that's just how he is," Katie said. "It's not like we've known him all that long. He could be one of those people that just acts differently."

"True," said Regan.

"I don't want to talk about this anymore," said Rya. "I'm tired. Let's just go home."

And home they went, riding on their dragons through the starry night sky. But even though they hadn't continued their conversation, Regan couldn't shake the feeling that something was wrong.

The next morning they woke up to find the kill pile restocked. They ate a quick meal of the bacon and sausage-like meats they'd discovered. Emma had grown quite good at preparing them. After they were finished they left to go meet with Derrick.

"What do you think'll happen?" Rya asked Regan as they soared over the rust-colored landscape.

"What do you mean?"

"Like, do you think we'll make any changes to the plan or anything?"

Regan shrugged. "I think it's already a solid battle plan. I can't think of anything we'd want to change." Apparently satisfied, Rya turned back to her dragon to watch the passing volcanos that were erupting. Lava spewed up and out of them, like giant fountains.

Rya sighed, "They are pretty aren't they?"

"Yeah, I guess they are. In a dangerous sort of way," Emma replied. After that they didn't speak, just watched in silence as the fiery lava trickled down the volcano's sides.

Eventually they reached the camp's volcano. Landing once again in the clearing, they walked around the giant mountain to Derrick's house. Once they reached the giant stone outcropping, they walked to the far side of the structure where the faint path they'd followed the first time they'd visited him was.

"I hope the battle is soon," Rya remarked when they first stepped onto the trail.

Regan glanced at her, her eyebrows raised, "Why? Don't you want more time to prepare?"

Rya shrugged. "Well, yeah. But then I have less time to be nervous."

"They say that the waiting is the hardest part," Emma put in.

"Who is 'they?'" Regan asked.

"Like, everyone," Emma replied. Even though Regan didn't feel that they were right, she could see where they were coming from.

"Whatever. It's not really up to us anyway."

The conversation had lasted long enough for them to make it to Derrick's house. Swiftly, Katie walked up and rapped on the door.

"Hello?" she called. The door opened, and a stranger opened the door. The man was shorter than Katie, and skinny. His messy hair was a mousy brown color. His luminous blue eyes seemed too large for his small body, and his hands looked like tiny sticks stuck together.

"Oh, hello, girls!"

"Uh, hi?" Regan replied.

"Oh, I'm sorry, you probably don't know me. My name is Maverick." He gestured for them to come in. Cautiously, Katie led the way into the house, Regan close behind. Rya peered out from behind Regan's shoulder, and Emma followed behind them.

Inside they found Derrick seated on the leather chair, and two women were sitting on the couch across from him. Maverick left to the back of the house, where he picked something up. The four girls just stood in the doorway, watching.

"Ladies, please sit down." Derrick said. Just then Maverick came back, holding four large pillows. He set them down on the ground next to the couch and motioned for them to sit. Slowly, Regan settled herself down on the soft pillow, her friends doing the same.

"I hope you don't mind," Derrick continued, "I asked a few of my advisors to come. They help with all decisions." The two women smiled at them. One had long black hair and was wearing a bright yellow dress that came way past her knees. The other had red hair pulled into a bun. She was wearing a dark gray shirt with a black skirt. Regan noticed right away that the girl had very light colored eyes. They looked almost white.

"This is Bella," Derrick said pointing to the dark haired woman, who waved sweetly at them. "And this is Charlotte." She too waved at the four girls.

"Hi," Katie said, now sounding much more confident than before.

"Now that everyone is settled, shall we begin the discussion?" Derrick asked. Bella and Emma both nodded. "Alright then."

"When will the fight be?" Rya asked outright.

"That is the question, is it not?" Derrick said. "How about two weeks from now?"

"That's not gonna work," Regan told him. "By then they'll have the rocket built and launched!"

"Well, one week then," he said.

"Still too long," Emma replied. "It has to be sooner."

"Two days from now," Charlotte said abruptly. Derrick turned to her.

"Why then?"

With her chin turned up, she answered, "Because that gives us the time we need to prepare while not allowing too much time to get nervous or allow the Pride to finish their rocket." Maverick nodded.

"It makes sense," said Bella. Derrick didn't look happy about it, but eventually he relented.

"Okay, two days from now it is. Would you like to make any changes to the plan before we start preparations?"

Bella shook her head. "It's actually a really good plan. You can tell how much thought you girls put into it." Regan smiled inwardly, remembering how they'd come up with the plan only a few minutes before they'd presented it.

"So are we done here?" Rya asked. After glancing at each other, Bella and Maverick both nodded. Charlotte just glared at them. Derrick too gave a slow nod.

"It would seem so," he announced. "Thank you for joining us today ladies. We will see you tomorrow evening to make sure everything is ready."

"Sounds good," Emma replied. Gradually, all four girls made their way to their feet. Katie was the only one you waved goodbye, getting an excited wave from Maverick in response. Regan held the door open for her friends, watching the four adults as she did so. Once all three were outside, she followed them, closing the door behind her. Emma and Katie were waiting for her a little ways down the path where the trees started, Rya having already left to say hi to Lucas and Ace.

"That went well," Katie remarked when Regan caught up.

Emma nodded. "Better than I'd hoped," she replied.

Regan laughed, "That Maverick dude was kinda weird looking."

"Yeah," said Katie. "And Charlotte was kind of scary. Did you see the way she was looking at us? It's like she hated us or something."

"Don't be stupid," Emma replied. "How could she hate us? She barely knows us!"

"Still, she creeps me out."

"You gotta admit, Emma, those eyes were pretty strange," Regan said.

"True," Emma replied. "But you should never judge someone by how they look."

Regan nodded, "You're right. Now let's catch up to Rya."

Once they arrived at the outcropping they spotted Rya, Lucas, and Ace all seated around a small fire on the outskirts of camp. Katie saw them first and sprinted over to them. Emma ran too, leaving Regan by herself. Laughing at her friends' excitement, she jogged to join them.

"What's up?" she asked when she reached them.

"Nothing much," Lucas replied.

"Rya told us about the meeting," Ace informed them. He was seated on a small rock. Regan wasn't sure how he fit, being that the rock was smaller than the ones Rya and Lucas were seated on and that he was not a small boy. It almost looked like he was about to fall off.

"So, two days," Lucas said. "I can't tell if I'm excited or scared."

"To be honest," Regan replied, "me either."

"We've never fought before," Katie told them.

"Well, we have over who is doing the dishes and things," Rya laughed, "but nothing like an actual battle."

"Neither has the camp," Ace replied. He twiddled his thumbs.

"I'm excited," Emma stated proudly. "What do we have to fear? Sure they have those big guards and all, but look at us! We have dragons!"

"She has a good point," Regan conceded.

"Plus, we have a whole camp of people," Katie added.

"Not everyone in the camp is able to fight though," Lucas argued.

"Not everyone in the Pride will fight either," Katie said back. "Some of them might even side with us!"

"Another good point," Regan smiled.

"Why don't we enjoy the day?" Rya asked. "It could be our last together."

Regan stared at her, stunned. She hadn't considered the fact that one of them might die. Sure, she knew there were deaths in a battle. But she hadn't thought about one of those dead being her friend. Suddenly, she became very nervous about the outcome of the battle.

"That's a good idea," she said finally. With grim nods, the others agreed.

"We should all hang out at our dome," Emma suggested. This lightened the mood a little.

"Yes! That sounds like so much fun!" Rya exclaimed.

"But then we'd have to walk back," Ace said.

"We'll bring you back on the dragons," Emma replied.

With smiles the boys left to go ask their moms if they could go with the girls. They came back with even bigger smiles.

"They said yes!" Ace told them excitedly.

Katie gave a fist pump, "Oh yeah!" she said.

"But they said we have to be back by tonight so we can sleep and help with preparations tomorrow since we'll miss helping today," Lucas told them.

"That's not a problem," Rya replied.

"Let's go now so we have more time," Emma said. She raced Lucas to the clearing, Ace and Katie running happily behind them. Rya ran too. Regan hesitated.

"What's wrong?" Rya asked. She'd come back after seeing Regan wasn't following.

"You said this might be our last day together," she answered, her head down.

"Yeah, so?"

"We might die."

"And?" Rya asked. "We could die any day. I could die right now."

"But, there's a higher chance of us dying in the fight." Regan looked up at her friend, tears barely held back. "What if you die? Or Katie? Or Emma? What if I never see any of you again? Life would be miserable if you were. . . gone."

Rya paused to think before saying, "Everything is going to be fine. No one's going to die. We have the dragons, remember? If we aren't there to protect each other, the dragons will be."

Regan, feeling reassured, wiped away a tear. "Yeah, I guess you're right."

"I always am," Rya smiled.

"Not true," Regan said back, smiling back at her best friend. Before Rya could continue to argue, they saw Lucas pop out from the tree line where their friends had disappeared earlier.

"You guys coming?" he shouted.

Regan turned to Rya. "Race ya."

"Hey!" Rya shouted after her, "That's not fair! You got a head start!"

Regan laughed.

When they reached the clearing they found Katie seated on Angel's back and Emma trying desperately to hoist Ace up onto Nakata.

"About time you guys got here," she said through gritted teeth. "Get over here and help me."

"Why doesn't he just run up her wing like I do with Nyx?" Regan asked.

"Because this guy is too clumsy and heavy!" she replied sharply.

"Hey!" Ace called down. He only reached about halfway up Nakata's side, and he was standing on Emma's shoulders. Emma herself was crouched down with the effort. "It's not my fault; I'm bigger than you!"

"Hold on," Regan told them. She hurried over and bent down next to Emma so their shoulders were level. "Ace, put your foot on me."

Obediently, the boy put his foot onto Regan's shoulder. With a portion of the weight taken off, Emma was able to stand a little taller. Regan stood to match her friend's height.

"Can you reach yet?" Emma asked him.

"Not yet," he replied. "I'm still half a foot off."

"Alright, let's shove him," Regan said.

Ace glanced down. "Wait, what?"

Before he could say another word, Emma and Regan put all their strength into pushing him onto the dragon.

"Ah!"

Regan looked up to see Ace sprawled on his stomach on Nakata's back. His arms hung over one side while his legs hung over the other. With a grunt he pulled his legs over to straddle the large dragon's back.

"Thanks," he told them sarcastically.

Regan raised an eyebrow, "You're up there aren't you?"

"Well, yeah," he conceded.

"Okay, then."

"Lemme show you how it's done," Rya said. She signaled to Nakata, who in turn put her wing down to act as a ramp. Gracefully, Rya sprinted up to set herself down in front of Ace.

Ace stared at her, dumbfounded, "Dang."

Regan rolled her eyes. "Showoff."

"Let's see you do better," countered Rya.

"Fine."

Nyx let his wing down, covering much more space as he was a lot bigger than Nakata.

Regan motioned for Lucas, who stared at her in confusion, "What?"

"Follow me," she replied.

"But, I've never done this before."

"Dude, it's really not that hard. Just run as fast as you can up his wing. Worst case scenario, you slide back down," Regan said quietly so Rya couldn't hear.

"Fine," Lucas answered, although his blue eyes still held that same wary light.

Regan counted down, "Three, two, one, go."

With that they were off, Regan sprinting, Lucas not far behind. When she got to the top, Regan swung her leg over, ending up in her usual riding position, and immediately reached back over to help pull Lucas to the top. Smoothly he sat himself behind her.

"How's that?" she asked Rya with a smirk.

"Decent," Rya replied.

"Decent?" Ace asked, his eyes wide. "That was way better than decent! Go, Lucas!"

"Hey, what about me?" said Regan.

"Are we leaving yet?" Emma said before anyone could reply, "Or are we going to keep sitting here on dragons and talking?" Angel and Ember were already braced for takeoff.

"Yeah, yeah," Regan replied. "c'mon Nyx, let's go."

"Just don't go too fast, okay?" Lucas said.

"Where's the fun in that?" Regan replied. "Hey, guys, last one to the dome is a rotten egg!"

With that, Nyx was off. His giant wings propelled them up into the sky. Regan grabbed onto the dragon's giant horns for a handhold. The wind hit her in the face like a hammer, making her eyes water. The sky was blush colored, and the scattered clouds a darker burgundy. She looked back at Lucas, who was gripping her around the waist tightly.

"You okay back there?"

"Never better." His eyes were shut.

"Open your eyes, Lucas. It's pretty up here."

He opened them, "Woah."

"Just don't look down," Regan laughed, interrupting the action he had already started. He stopped and glanced at her.

"Good idea," he said eventually.

Regan leaned to one side so she could look around Lucas to Nakata, who was behind them. The green dragon's scales glistened like a jewel in the bright sunlight.

"How's Ace doing?" she called. She saw Rya's head peek over Nakata's enormous head.

"He's such a scaredy cat! He won't even open his eyes!"

"C'mon, Ace!" Lucas yelled back. "It's awesome!"

Regan laughed, "How'd you figure that out?"

Ace must've opened his eyes, because a few seconds later they heard a loud, "Woah!"

"Told ya!" Lucas said. Regan checked again to see the placings. Nyx was easily in first, Nakata a close second, Ember and Angel side by side.

"We still have a ways to go," Regan said to herself.

"Can he go any faster?" Lucas asked.

"I thought you didn't want to go fast."

"Well, I don't want to be a rotten egg do I?" He smiled.

"No," she replied with a similar grin. "I guess not."

"So how do we get him to go faster?" he asked.

"Ask him."

Lucas's eyebrows furrowed, "He understands us?"

"Seems to," she replied. "Whenever I ask for something he does it."

"Okay, then." He leaned slightly to one side. "Hey, Nyx? Can we go faster? We don't want to lose the ra-"

He hadn't even finished his sentence before Nyx was off like a bullet. Regan and Lucas held on for their lives, laughing the entire way.

Nyx claimed first in the race by a landslide. Nakata was second, Angel surprisingly followed her in third. Last came Ember, huffs of smoke spewing from his nostrils.

"Looks like Ember over here is not a fast flier," Rya laughed.

"It's not his fault. He got overheated," Emma told them.

"Are you okay?" Katie asked, remembering the last time the flame drake had gotten too hot.

"Yep, I'm fine. Most of it came out in smoke," she replied. In confirmation a giant plume of smoke escaped from the red dragon's mouth. Ember made a coughing noise, then seemed to settle down.

"Is he okay?" Katie asked.

"He should be fine. I think he's just tired."

"Well, what should we do first?" Rya asked excitedly. She began walking toward the dome.

"Good question," Regan said, following behind her friend.

"Why don't you give us a tour of the place?" Ace suggested when they entered the dome.

"There's not much to see," Emma replied. "Back there is the bedroom, the bathroom, and an empty room that we put the containers in. Up here is the kitchen and living room. That's basically it."

"Have you explored any of those other domes?" Lucas asked.

"Actually, no, we haven't," Katie replied.

"That gives me an idea!" Rya burst out. "We should make a fort!"

"A fort?" Regan scoffed.

"Yeah! We can pick one of the domes and build it into a fort."

"Won't that take more than one day?" Katie asked.

"Maybe," Rya answered. "But we can finish it after the fight." She glanced at Regan, who smiled.

"Sounds like fun," Regan consented.

"Okay," Lucas said. "Let's go find us a fort!"

They ended up picking a dome near the edge of the cluster of buildings. It was only a couple minutes walking between the two domes. After walking inside, they saw the same setup they had in the girls' home; a kitchen and living room when you walk in, and a giant bedroom, a bathroom, and an extra room in the back. They all had the same ugly coloring as well.

"So, what do we want to do first?" Emma prompted.

"We could set up the sleeping areas in the back," Ace said.

"Okay," Regan replied, leading the way to the back of the house from where they were standing in the living room. The back bedroom only had four beds, and there wasn't much space to add in two more with space to walk around them.

"Well, this is a problem," Rya stated.

"This is supposed to be a fort, right? It doesn't have to be livable. It just has to be fun to hang out in," Regan replied.

"True," Lucas said.

"How are we supposed to have fun here with all the walls?" Ace asked.

"We can remove the walls," Emma said, catching on to Regan's thought train.

"And we can bring more mattresses in here so the whole room is like a giant bed," Regan added.

"Sounds like a lot of work," Rya complained.

"We have time. Besides, working with you guys is fun," Regan said.

"Better than working with my mom," Ace agreed.

"How are we going to take down the walls though?" Katie asked.

"We could throw rocks at it?" Lucas said, although rather unsure.

"I don't think that'll work," Emma said.

"We need something like a hammer," Rya said.

"I think I have one," Regan said excitedly.

"Why would you have a hammer?" Emma asked, her eyebrows furrowed.

"I'm pretty sure I brought one in the suitcases we had when we first came," she replied. Rya rolled her eyes.

"Trust Regan to bring a hammer in a suitcase."

Regan sprang to her own defense, "Hey, you never know when you might need one."

"So we can take the walls down, but we still need mattresses," Emma stated.

"Easy," Ace said confidently. "If all the domes are the same, like this one and yours, shouldn't there be mattresses in those? We can just carry them from a different one into here."

"Smart," Katie said.

"Okay, I'm going to go get the hammer so we can start taking the walls down. We should think about finding a broom too. Since they're concrete it'll probably make a mess," Regan said.

"I'll look for a broom," Lucas replied. "Do you guys want to start carrying mattresses? We can stack them in the living room for now until we get the walls dealt with."

"Sounds like a plan!" Emma said.

"You know, when I thought about building a fort, I figured it would be a blanket fort. Or something easy," Rya whined again.

"If this is to be our hang out spot while we're here, which will probably be a long time, do you really want it to be a blanket fort?" Emma asked.

"Well, no."

"Exactly. Now come help us."

Lucas was first out the door, heading for a nearby dome to look for the broom. Regan ran to the girls' home to grab the hammer, and the other four went to the closest building, which was only around one hundred feet away. Not far to walk.

Regan, out of breath after sprinting to their dome, rushed into her home and raced to the bedroom. She knelt down when she got to her bed and pulled out her suitcase from where she'd stuffed it under the bed.

"Here we go," she said finally after having thrown most of the clothes and things she'd had in the suitcase onto the floor. She pulled out a sledgehammer, the handle made of oak and the head of the hammer carbon steel painted red by her father. She smiled when she thought of him. Then, remembering the task at hand and not wanting to leave her friends waiting too long, she stuffed all her clothes back into the suitcase and shoved it closed. She zipped it shut, pushed it back under the bed, and was back out the door. Running with a hammer wasn't the best idea, which she knew, but at the moment she didn't care.

When she arrived back at the dedicated fort dome, she saw Lucas waiting at the front door with a broom that reminded Regan of the brooms ridden by witches in movies. Looking around, she couldn't find any of the others.

"Where's everyone else?" she asked. He pointed to the dome she'd seen them enter when she left. Only Emma was visible, carrying the mattress vertically. The other three must've been inside on the other end of the mattress. They were, apparently, having trouble getting it through the doorway, even though the entrance itself was large and square.

"Can't be that hard, can it?" she wondered aloud.

"I keep hearing Ace yell that it's floppy," Lucas laughed.

"Should we go help them?" Regan asked with a smile.

He paused, then smiled, "Nah, it's too funny listening to them."

"Wanna help me with the walls then?" She lifted the sledgehammer from where it hung by her side to rest on her palm.

"Sure," he replied. He followed her into the dome. Stacked in the living room were four mattresses.

"You guys got a lot done," she remarked.

"Those are the ones from the bedroom," Lucas replied. "We thought it'd be a good idea to take them out before we started demolishing things."

"Smart," Regan said. She walked to the bedroom. They'd taken the curtains down as well, and now all that was left was a giant room and three walls separating areas. She walked up to the one on the left and took a swing with the sledgehammer. A small crack started to form.

"This might take a while," she said with a sigh.

It took them the rest of the morning to get all three walls down. The others, after having emptied the other house of mattresses, pitched in by hitting it with stone boulders the size of their hands. The boulders didn't do much, but Regan's swings with the sledgehammer helped immensely. The concrete walls were thin, and cracked easily. Lucas cleaned with the broom as soon as they got another wall down. The whole time they were working they joked and talked contentedly. They took a break around noon.

"Phew," said Rya, wiping sweat from her forehead, "that's hard work."

"No kidding," Regan replied. She set the head of the hammer on her shoulder.

"So, what's for lunch?" Ace asked.

"Whatever we want to make out of the kill pile," Emma answered.

"Kill pile?" Lucas inquired.

"Where the dragons put their prey," Regan replied. "They end up killing more than we need, and they dump it into a pile. Half the stuff ends up going bad."

"Oh."

"Let's go find something soon. I'm starving!" Rya exclaimed.

"I agree," said Katie.

"Okay, okay, calm down," Regan laughed. "We'll go get something to eat. Emma, are you okay with making it?"

"Yeah," Emma said.

"I'll help," Katie offered.

"Thanks," Emma replied. Regan dropped her sledgehammer, Lucas his broom, and the others the rocks they'd been using. Casually, Regan headed to the door, just to be pushed aside by a running Rya.

"C'mon, Regan, hurry up!"

"Jeez, Rya!" Regan laughed, hurrying to catch up with her friend. She ran out the door, Lucas right behind her laughing.

"Hey, slow down."

Regan turned to see Ace slogging behind them. He looked exhausted, which made sense. He'd done most of the work carrying the beds, being as strong as he was, and had still tried to help take down the concrete walls.

"Sorry," she said. She slowed down to a walk. Rya did, too.

"We're going to go on ahead and start cooking," Emma told them when she jogged past. Katie jogged beside her.

"Okay," Lucas said. They lost sight of them after the two girls passed behind a building. They had to weave around the buildings because there wasn't a set path going through them.

"So when we get back, are we going to move the mattresses?" Lucas asked.

"Probably, yeah," Regan answered. "We can finish the bedroom today and then work on the rest after the battle."

"How do you think the battle will go?" Ace asked.

"What do you mean?" Regan dodged the question. Even though she was confident in the dragons' ability to protect them, it didn't make her want to talk about the battle any more.

"Like, do you think Ann and Brian will fight? Or do you think they'll make those big security guards do it?"

"I don't know," she responded.

"I don't think they're going to fight," Rya put in. "They're too stuck up for that."

"I bet they will," Lucas said. "They'll probably get mad at us and lose their tempers."

"Maybe," said Regan.

"Will your parents even let you guys fight?" Rya asked the boys. Lucas shrugged.

"I sure hope so."

"Yeah, I want to kick some butt!" Ace exclaimed, emphasizing with a fist pump.

"Me, too!" Rya agreed. She faked a punch and a kick. "I know karate."

"No, you don't," Regan laughed. "The only fighting you've ever done is wrestling with your brothers."

"Okay, maybe I don't know karate," she admitted, "but I can fight!"

Just then they arrived at the dome. A savory aroma greeted them as they walked through the door. Inside they saw Emma cooking something on the stove, and Katie starting to set the table.

"Mmm, that smells really good!" Lucas praised.

"Thanks. We decided to cook one of the chicken-looking things," Emma told them.

"Didn't you have to pluck it?" Regan asked. Along with butchering hogs, she'd also helped butcher chickens at her grandpa's farm.

"No, they didn't have any feathers," Katie replied. "They must have adapted since they didn't need them anymore."

"Or they adapted because the feathers kept catching on fire," Rya said.

"Or that," Katie laughed.

"What are chicken's wings for anyway?" Rya asked. "They can't fly."

"Actually, I'm pretty sure they can fly," Regan replied. Rya looked at her funny.

"You're kidding."

"No."

"Can we eat yet?" Ace interrupted. "All this talk about chickens is making me even hungrier!"

"It's almost ready," Emma told them. "You guys can help Katie set the table. It should be ready when you're done."

"I already have the plates out. We just need forks, water, and napkins," Katie said.

"I call getting water," Regan said loudly.

"I'll get the napkins," Rya said, already on her way to the cabinet where they stored the napkins. Regan pointed to a drawer on the other side of the kitchen, next to the ugly fridge.

"There's the silverware, if you want to get forks," she said to Ace. The big boy nodded.

"I can help you with the water, Regan," Lucas offered. Regan nodded, grabbed six plastic cups that had been sitting on the counter, and walked out the door to the stream. She knelt down next to it and dipped the cups, one by one, into the clear, fresh water. The first three cups she handed to Lucas, who stood beside her. The last three she kept so that he wouldn't have to carry all of them.

Once all the cups were full they went back inside. There they found Katie, Rya, and Ace all sitting at the small table that was set with blue plastic plates, pink napkins, and bright green silverware. Ace's chair looked way too small for him.

"Why so colorful?" Lucas asked.

"We ran out of paper plates and clear silverware," Rya told them, "the napkins were just for fun."

"Oh."

"Lunch is served!" Emma said then. She dropped another blue plate in the middle of the table, this one piled with the chicken she'd been cooking. The outside of the bird was a delicious, golden brown. With a small knife, Emma divided the animal into equal pieces.

After the animal was cut, she gave each person a piece on their plates. Rya and Regan both sat on the footstool, the two boys and Katie sat in the chairs, and Emma shoved one of the chairs from the living room to the table and sat on that. There was barely enough room for all the plates on the small table, but they made it work.

"You know," Rya said while chewing on a chunk of chicken, "I've never done work like this with my friends. But, it's fun."

"Yeah," Ace replied, "I never do this much exercise, even when my mom tries to make me."

THE PRIDE

Lucas laughed, "He really doesn't."

"Well, I guess we're a special case," Regan chuckled. She shoveled a forkful of the meat into her mouth. "This is amazing."

"Thank you," Emma replied, beaming. Along with the chicken, they had a bowl full of the square, seedless berries. The sweet fruit complemented the savory chicken nicely.

They continued the meal, joking and talking the entire time. Most of the conversation involved talk about the dragons, the camp, and NASA. The two boys were extremely curious about the organization. They talked about it while they were cleaning up. Rya and Lucas threw away the plates, while Ace and Katie washed and dried the cups, and put them away. Emma and Regan cleaned up and put away all the leftovers.

"So, NASA sent you guys here as an experiment?" Lucas asked with his eyebrows furrowed.

"Yep," Rya replied.

"And your parents aren't here?" Ace inquired.

"No, they aren't," Emma said.

"So this whole time you've been by yourselves?" Lucas asked.

Regan responded, "Yeah..."

"Have you seen any adults around?" Rya asked him. He shook his head.

"No."

"So, wasn't it kinda obvious?" Regan replied.

"I guess, yeah," Lucas said. "I just didn't think they'd send unsupervised kids to an unknown planet."

"I think maybe we were supposed to have adults with us, but they all went to the other dome settlement," Regan explained.

"Where's that?" Ace asked.

"Isn't it on the other side of the planet?" Katie said, asking for confirmation, which she got in the form of a Regan nod.

"Yeah, they wanted to see if the entire planet was good for a settlement or if it was just one certain place they could put people."

"I'm fairly sure the whole planet is fine," Lucas replied. "The animals that landed here turned out fine." By now they were done cleaning up and started walking back out to the dome they were using for their fort.

"Yeah, didn't you guys get here after a rocket crash landed?" Emma asked.

"Yeah," Ace replied.

"Well, we didn't, our ancestors did," Lucas corrected. "But that was a while ago. My great grandparents were the first to come here." They passed the dragon's nest and headed right, in the direction of the fort.

"Are you guys ever going to see your parents again?" Ace asked. "I can't imagine not seeing my mom every day."

Regan remembered all the nights she'd spent lying awake, thinking about her parents and siblings. All the nights she'd woken up homesick, wishing for her blue bed and the red barn, and her two sisters. Hoping that soon she'd see all of them again.

"We'll see them again," she answered finally. She almost had to choke out the words, a wave of homesickness crashing into her. She remembered the battle. What would happen if she died? She'd never get to see her family again. She'd never feel the tight hug of her mother, or hear the monotone singing of her father that made everyone laugh. She'd never play with her sisters and fight over who did the dishes. Silently, she made a promise. She would not die. She would see her family again. And she would make sure her friends saw their families too.

Seeing Regan was finished talking, Emma explained further. "NASA is working on a transportation system. They already have a mail system set up. It can only deliver mail one way though, and that's from here to there. Supposedly it's for sending back information, but I just use it to send things to my family. We can tell them all about our adventures when they actually visit us."

"That sounds cool!" Lucas said. By now they had reached their destination. Katie entered first through the square cut door, Emma and Lucas following on her heels. Ace went next, Rya and Regan side by side behind him. They made their way to the back room once more.

"Let's move the hammer and rocks out of here first," Emma said. Regan nodded and bent down to retrieve her hammer. Everyone else picked up the rock they'd been using, except for Katie.

Lucas grabbed her rock and said, "I can carry this out if you want to finish sweeping."

"That's good with me. I like cleaning," Katie smiled. Lucas grinned back. Emma led the way to the front door, where she promptly stepped outside and dropped the rock she'd been holding onto the ground to the left of the door.

"Just pile them here?" she asked.

"Yeah," Rya said, dropping hers as well. "That way if we need to destroy more walls later we can just use these."

Nodding, Ace plopped his down next to the two girls' rocks. "Makes sense to me." Regan leaned her sledgehammer against the wall, and Lucas placed his rock on the top of the pile.

"So now we carry in the mattresses," Lucas said, making it sound more like a question than a statement.

"Yep," Regan replied. As a group they went back inside. Katie was waiting for them, a dustpan full of concrete chunks in one hand and the broom in the other.

"I found this in the bathroom. Handy, right?"

"Lucky find," Emma replied. Katie left to dump the concrete outside while Lucas, Ace, and Rya headed over to one of the beds. Together, the three kids easily lifted the bed. They didn't have nearly as much trouble as they did the first time they moved it, probably because they didn't have to lift it vertically. Instead they kept it flat. They carried it through the large, open hallway into the bedroom. There they laid it on the floor, shoving it smoothly into one corner. It filled up one eighth of the space needed to cover the entire floor.

"How many beds did you bring in? Other than the ones you took from this bedroom," Regan asked Ace when they were done laying out the first mattress.

"Four," he answered. "We only emptied one house."

"I think that'll be perfect," she replied. Turned out she was right. They managed to fit five mattresses along the back wall, their short end facing them when they stood in the hallway. The last three beds they placed along the wall closest to them, although they had to rotate them to get them to fit. It was almost dark when they got done. Time for them to take the boys home. Together, all six kids plopped onto the mattresses in exhaustion, but the feeling of accomplishment they all felt was worth it.

"Ah, man!" said Ace. "I don't wanna go home!"

"Me either," said Lucas. "It's been too much fun hanging out with you guys."

"Yeah," said Rya, "but we'll get to see you tomorrow, too! Derrick told us to come over tomorrow night to make sure everything was ready."

"True," Lucas replied, "and I guess we do have the battle. I can't believe that's in two days!"

"Technically it's a day and a half. A night only counts as half a day," Emma corrected him.

"Even sooner," Lucas said.

Slowly, Regan sat up, "Well, I guess we better get you guys back," she said. Lucas nodded and moved to sit up as well. Gradually, all six kids got up and trudged toward the door. Although they'd had fun carrying the beds and smashing walls, it was tough work, and all of them were exhausted.

They walked down to the dragons' nest. Once again, Regan and Emma helped Ace get on Nakata, although it took a little longer since they were tired. Regan and Lucas had a little more trouble with mounting Nyx. Regan's arms felt like lead, and pulling Lucas up after her was a struggle. She managed it, however, and eventually everyone was seated on a dragon. The dragons, having slept almost the entire day, were nowhere near as exhausted as their owners. They seemed almost anxious to take off.

"Alright," Rya said mid-yawn, "let's go."

The dragons lifted off in a flash. Regan, who had slouched comfortably at first, remembered just before they took off to hold onto Nyx's horns. She was lucky, because Nyx shot like a bullet off the ground and flew straight up into the dark red sky. Lucas held onto Regan tightly, almost squeezing the breath out of her. She didn't say anything though, and loosened his grip after they straightened out. Regan's eyes streamed water, the wind so forceful that she thought if she let go she would go flying off Nyx's back.

The journey ended quickly, and soon they arrived at the camp. Instead of landing in the clearing this time, they touched down near the edge of the camp so Lucas and Ace wouldn't have to walk as far to get to their house. A few people noticed them, but instead of fear all that greeted the dragons was awe. It was a step up from the kid's reactions.

"Bye, guys," Lucas said as he slid down Nyx's wing, "see you tomorrow!"

"Yeah," yelled Ace. His attempt at using Nakata's wing as a slide wasn't quite as graceful as Lucas's. "See you tomorrow!"

"Bye!" the girls called back. As soon as the boys were gone they took off again, this time slower. The dragons must have figured out how tired they were because this flight felt more like they were soaring. Regan almost wanted to let go of Nyx's horns and reach her hands out. But she resisted the urge, instead clinging safely to his horns. They didn't talk much on the way back, conversation replaced by numerous yawns.

When they got back to the dome, they slid off their dragons and went straight to their beds. Regan was asleep almost as soon as she pulled the blankets over her.

"Goodnight," she managed to say before she drifted off to sleep.

Chapter 10

The next morning when Regan woke up, everyone else was still asleep. She groggily flicked off the covers and got out of bed. She went outside to see if the dragons were still there and saw that the sun was fairly high in the sky. *Almost noon,* she thought. She couldn't be certain, however, as she didn't have her pocket watch with her. She'd left it on Rya's suitcase one night, which she used as a nightstand, to use for a clock. Rya had a tendency to wake up late, and then decide it was too early and go back to bed. The pocket watch was a reminder that her friends were waiting for her to get up.

Regan went back inside and pulled out the leftover chicken from the fridge. They'd skipped supper last night in favor of sleeping, and although chicken wasn't really a breakfast-type food, she was starving. Besides, they didn't have anything else to eat. She opened the red container that held the chicken and placed it into the microwave, setting the timer for one minute. They didn't use the microwave much, as they either finished all the meat they cooked or gave the leftovers to the dragons.

When the microwave beeped to signal the time was up, she opened it to release a flood of steam. She waved it off and sat the container of chicken on the table. She went to grab another one of the blue plates, and upon seeing Emma walk out of the hallway, grabbed two. Emma was rubbing her eyes and yawning loudly.

"What time is it?" she asked. Regan set the two plates on the table and grabbed two forks.

"Almost noon, I think," she answered, "I didn't check the watch though."

That seemed to wake Emma up, "Almost noon!"

"Yeah," Regan replied.

"We better get the other two up then," Emma said.

"Why?" Regan asked. She gave Emma a fork and then sat down to eat.

"So we can start getting ready for the battle. We can't just walk in with no weapons or anything and just expect to win."

"True," Regan replied. She stood up again. "You go wake them up. I'll get more plates."

Emma nodded and left to go get their friends. When she came back, Rya was whining about how early it was and Katie was just rubbing her eyes, yawning. Regan had already set out the extra plates and forks, and was sitting down again eating. Katie sat down next to her with another yawn.

"Why chicken?" Rya asked when she saw what Regan was eating.

"Because it's good and it was all we had," she replied. Rya shrugged and sat down.

"It's food, I guess." With that she dug in. The plateful of chicken was gone in a matter of seconds.

"You must've been hungry," Regan remarked. Rya nodded and stood up to throw her plate in their small trash can on the other side of the fridge.

"Starving," she replied. The rest of them finished eating quickly and handed Rya their plates to throw away. After they cleaned everything up and put the extra meat away, they headed outside to check on the dragons.

"If the dragons are here, we should take a look around and see if there's anything we can make a weapon out of," Emma said. At this Regan paused and stood outside the door.

"Do I really need to make a weapon?" Regan asked. "I have a sledgehammer."

"Maybe you don't. But what are we going to use? You don't have three extra sledgehammers," she paused. "Do you?"

"No," Regan said. "I have a bat though."

Rya stared at her. "Why the heck would you have a bat?"

"Well, we did play softball together that one year, remember?" Katie said.

"Yeah," Rya replied.

"I brought it just in case you wanted to play," Regan told her. Rya rolled her eyes.

"Regan, when was the last time we played softball together?"

"Uh," Regan hesitated, "two years ago?"

"More like four," Rya corrected.

"Rya, be grateful she brought it. Now we only have to make two weapons," Emma said.

"Who's going to use the bat?" Katie asked.

"I vote Regan," said Rya.

"I'm using the sledgehammer," Regan said. "And we all know you were the best hitter on the team. I say Rya uses the bat."

"I was pretty good," Rya remembered with a smile. "Alright, I'll use the bat. But we still have to find weapons for Emma and Katie."

"Do you think the camp would have some we could borrow?" Katie asked. Regan shook her head.

"They have enough on their hands making weapons for themselves. We can handle making two."

"Let's just go take a look around," Emma said. "If we don't find anything we can use chunks of concrete or something."

"Okay," Rya agreed. After having stood near the entrance to the dome talking, they continued on their path to the dragons' nest. Upon entering, they found the four dragons chasing a tiny mouse-like creature. Their giant claws dwarfed the small animal, but it was so fast that whenever they tried to grab it, it would slip through their claws and run.

The mouse was running towards Nyx when they walked in, and he almost managed to snatch it. However, he trapped it underneath his clawed foot, and when he picked it up to see if he'd caught it, the mouse sprinted out as fast as its little legs would carry it. Nyx looked for it again, but he couldn't find it. With a flap of his wings he lifted himself up into the air to have a better vantage point. The gust of wind he made when he did so caused the mouse to go flying in the air, right into Ember's waiting mouth.

Ember chewed for a second, then spit out the animal's bones onto the ground. With an angry snort, Nyx flapped over to Ember and batted him on the snout. Nakata and Angel were shoving the flame drake around too. Ember blew a plume of fire to get them away. Nyx stuttered back and shook his head, his golden eyes narrowed. He was about to charge at Ember when Regan interrupted him.

"Nyx, quit messing around! We have exploring to do!" Regan shouted. With a final angry roar at Ember, Nyx trotted over and nudged Regan gently with his head.

"There's other mice out there," she told him, stroking his scaly head affectionately. He purred.

"Hey, quit fighting!" Katie shouted. Regan looked up to see her small friend rush into the midst of the three dragons, her hands held up.

"Katie, don't!" Emma yelled. But she was too late. Katie was already in between the three dragons, ice, fire, and leaves swirling around her in tornado-like wind gusts.

A second later, the air cleared. Katie stood in the center of the nest, her hands still held up. Ember, Angel, and Nakata had backed up, giving Katie space. The dragons' eyes were wide, making them look almost scared.

"Do you think they're scared of her?" Rya whispered through the tension. Regan shook her head.

"I think they're scared of hurting her." Regan walked toward Katie and patted her once on the back. "Nice work."

Katie smiled, "All I did was run in and yell at them to stop."

"Well, it worked," said Emma, who had joined them in the circle of dragons. Nyx added himself to the circle, snorting and pawing at the ground. Regan went back to Nyx and waited for him to set his wing down so she could get on his back. Katie was starting to pull herself up onto Angel, and Rya was heading over to Nakata.

"So, what are we looking for?" Rya asked. She ran up Nakata's wing and got herself settled on her back.

"I'm not sure exactly. Anything that looks like it would make a good club maybe. Like a strong branch," Emma answered. Rya nodded. Nyx finally noticed Regan waiting and lowered his wing. She promptly ran up and grabbed his horns, seating herself gracefully on his back.

"We'd better get going, seeing as we've wasted half the day sleeping," Regan stated, looking pointedly at Rya. Rya didn't notice, which was probably a good thing. Emma nodded, and Ember took off with a few giant flaps of his red wings. Smoke still curled from the tips of the crown of spikes on his head. Angel followed him, the remnants of the fight visible in the frosty air surrounding her. After Angel came Nakata, who barely showed any signs she had been fighting. The only way you could've told would have been to look at her eyes, which still gleamed in a livid way. She did a good job of disguising her lingering anger, however, as for the entire ride they had no more problems with the dragons fighting.

Nyx seemed, in contrast to Nakata, quite happy. He made mice with his powers, dark cloudlike animals. He chased them through the sky, happily roaring when he caught one and bit down on it, but confused when he didn't actually taste anything.

The girls didn't really talk on the flight. Every now and then one of them cracked a joke about something they saw below, but for the majority of it they sat in silence. They were either intent upon looking for something to fashion weapons out of or lost in their own thoughts. Regan was the latter.

She kept remembering the promise she had made to herself. She looked to her right, where Rya flew on Nakata, her head down, short blond hair covering her face. Then she looked to her left to see Katie seated on Angel. The small girl sat confidently on the dragonet's back. Then, she looked to the front, where Emma led the group. Her friend's pale skin and light blond hair stood out against the bright red sky. She reminded Regan of a doll. But beneath Emma's surface, Regan knew that she was a fiercely loyal friend. Emma would never let any of them come to danger. And neither would Regan.

These were the thoughts that ran through Regan's head when they spotted the Pride's cave.

"Oh no," Emma said loudly.

"What?" Rya asked. Then they all looked down. Thankfully, no one was outside the cave. Just being spotted could ruin the whole plan.

"Let's get out of here," Katie said quickly, her eyes wide.

"Wait," Regan replied. "We should go visit them."

Emma gaped at her, "Are you mad?"

"No, seriously," Regan continued. "Won't they be suspicious if we just walk in there tomorrow and start asking questions? We haven't seen them since we met the boys."

Rya thought about it. "You know, she has a good point."

"See? We don't have to stay long."

Still, Emma hesitated. "But, remember what happened last time we came? They kicked us out."

"Not necessarily," Regan replied. "Brian actually offered to give us a tour. I was the one who said we should leave." Finally, Emma gave in.

"Alright, fine," she said. "But nobody go and ask questions. At least, not suspicious ones."

"Wasn't planning on it," said Rya with a grin. "Let's go into the lion's den."

Chapter 11

They landed outside the cave, making sure the dragons knew to wait for them before they went in. The tunnel looked almost the same as it had the last time they'd visited, the difference being that torches now hung not only in the cavern the tunnel led to but in the tunnel itself. Helped by the light of the torches, Regan found her footing easily. Rya was leading the way to the cavern, Katie and Emma behind her. Regan brought up the rear. After making it to the surprisingly empty cavern, they walked cautiously to the smaller cave where they knew Ann and Brian's office was. Rya was the first to reach the entrance. She knocked on the large, wooden door. It was opened by Brian, his red dreadlocks in a mess around his head, his brown eyes looking worried. Upon seeing who it was though, he smiled.

"Hi! It's been so long since we've seen you! Where have you been?"

"I know right!" Rya replied. "We got really busy making this cool fort at home and we never had time to visit."

"This whole time you've been making a fort?" Ann came into view. Brian opened the door farther and let them into the office. Regan was pleased to see that the camera was still in place. She had to really stare at it to spot it though, and Ann caught her looking

"Yep," Rya answered excitedly. "It's really cool."

"I see," Ann said back, her eyes narrowed.

"You guys still up for that tour?" Brian asked. Regan nodded.

"Totally! How do you guys find your way around this place? That first cave is huge!"

"Everyone that lives here was born here," Brian replied. "So basically they've learned it since birth."

"Makes sense," Katie stated. They followed him out to the cave where the cafeteria was, where they had met Amanda and her husband. There were fewer people there than last time, most likely because lunch had already taken place.

"Of course, this is the cafeteria, which you have already seen," Brian said to them. He pointed toward the metal door Wesley had been protecting. "That is the security room. We can't go in there though."

"Why not?" Rya asked, ever curious.

Brian went to speak, but Ann interrupted him, "Because we said so."

Rya paused for a minute, then shrugged. "Okay!" Regan saw Emma and Katie share an amused glance. They were letting Rya do most of the talking. Regan was impressed with her acting skills. *She should've gone out for the school play last year,* she laughed in her head. Regan then noticed a small wooden doorway off to the right of where they stood in the middle of the room. She pointed to it.

"What's in there?"

Once again, Brian went to speak, but Ann stopped him before he could say anything.

"Oh, nothing. Just a little project we're working on." She smiled at them.

"Can we see it?" Katie asked innocently. Ann viciously shook her head, then smiled again.

"Sorry, but no," she told them. Brian waved them toward the other end of the cafeteria, where another wooden door sat. This one was a darker red than the door on the right, and it was much bigger, too.

"This leads to the hallway connected to all of our dorm rooms and training areas," he said as he turned the black, round handle and opened the door for them.

Regan's eyebrows furrowed. "Training areas? What are you training for?"

Brian's brown eyes lit up. "Many things. The guards are trained for battle, obviously, but we also have classrooms that teach our children to read and write, as well as draw. The kids can pick from many different categories of learning."

"Ooh, sounds fun!" Rya replied. "So you don't force them to learn anything they don't want to learn?"

Ann looked confused, "Why would we do that?"

"At schools back on Earth they had a few mandatory classes, like science and math," Emma explained. Ann nodded.

"Ah, I see."

"Can we see some of the rooms?" Rya asked. Brian nodded, and proceeded to show them both a girls and boys dormitory. Both looked rather plain, with just two pairs of carved stone bunk beds, one on each side of the room, for furniture. The walls were rough stone, as was the floor and ceiling, and light was provided by a lantern hanging from the ceiling in the middle of the room. Regan saw Rya wrinkle her nose when they walked into the rooms. She laughed quietly, until she thought about what it would be like to actually live there. Some people actually slept on these beds. She remembered their mission, but more importantly, she remembered Brian and Ann's plan.

"What happens if there's a family?" Katie asked as they exited the boys' dormitory. "Do they share a room?"

"No," Brian replied, "the babies are sent to a nursery farther down this hall, and the children get paired up to share a dormitory. The parents share rooms, but those are in a cavern separate from this one."

"Why don't you let the families share a room?" Emma inquired. Now they were headed even farther down the stone hallway.

"It is how it has always been done," Ann answered. "If it worked for our parents, grandparents, and great grandparents, it works for us."

So maybe they aren't evil, Regan thought, surprising herself. *Maybe they've just been taught wrong.*

Then, Brian walked up to yet another red-colored wood door and opened it.

"This," he said proudly, "is the guards' training room."

It was a large, circular cave with high ceilings. Stalactites hung from the roof of the cave, some lying broken on the ground. Stalagmites rose from the floor too, giant icicle looking structures. Fire blazed in braziers along the wall, protected from the rest of the room by thick panes of glass. A few guards were practicing in the cave. One of them, a big burly man with ratty red hair, held a dark metal sword, and while they were watching, he hacked at one of the stalagmites. After a few swings, the rock split into two, the top half sliding to the ground and shattering into even more pieces. The man turned to them. Regan thought she could feel the man's brown eyes peering into her soul.

"Well done, Victor!" Ann shouted, clapping her hands. The man bowed.

"Thank you, High One," he said in a gruff voice. With that he left, his large sword dragging on the ground. The screeching sound it made hurt Regan's ears, but Ann and Brian didn't seem to notice, so she said nothing.

"This place is huge!" Emma remarked. They stood in front of the door, gazing around at the dark cave. Although there was fire, it didn't emit much light. The light it did make only made it harder to see, with the stalagmites casting shadows everywhere. The fires also made the room really hot. In fact, Regan was already sweating.

"Yes," Ann said with a smile, "it is the biggest room we have. We take security very seriously here in the Pride." She turned to stare at Regan, as if challenging her to say something.

Regan took the challenge, "I can see that, but what are you protecting yourselves from?"

"Outsiders," Brian said. Ann punched him in the arm, then smiled at the girls.

"What outsiders?" Katie asked sweetly. "Aren't you the only people here, besides us?"

"Well, there's the people we kick out," Brian said, once again earning a punch from Ann. He rubbed his arm, grimacing as he did so.

"You kick people out?" Rya exclaimed. Ann glared at Brian, then nodded.

"Yes, but only the disobedient and disrespectful ones."

"What do you mean?" Emma asked. Ann motioned her head towards the door, and Brian led the way back to the main cavern.

"Well, some people decide not to follow the rules, or they think it's funny to talk rudely about my brother and I," she paused. "They need to be taught a lesson."

"So you send them away," Katie finished, "but, where do they go?"

Brian shook his head. "We don't know. And as long as we never see them again, we don't care either. They are a disgrace to the Pride."

Just then they arrived back at the main cavern.

"Tour's over," Ann said.

"But, we never saw the gardens!" Emma protested. Brian shook his head.

"I apologize, but my sister and I have some work to do. Maybe next time."

"Okay," Emma agreed.

"See you soon then?" Brian asked.

Regan smiled, "See you soon."

Chapter 12

They left the Pride joyfully. They hadn't given anything away, and Ann and Brian hadn't seemed suspicious of them. Overall, Regan thought the visit was a big success.

"Good job, Rya!" Regan applauded once they were high in the air, well out of earshot if you were standing on the ground. "Your acting was amazing!"

"Why, thank you!" Rya replied, giving a mock bow. The movement was slightly awkward, as she was seated on a giant green dragon.

"Mission complete," joked Emma.

"We still need to solve the problem of the weapons," Katie reminded them.

Regan nodded, "I don't think it should be too hard. Worst case scenario we can use the curtain rods from another dome."

"True," Emma replied. "I didn't think of that."

"Why don't we do that? I don't feel like riding around looking for trees anymore," Rya asked.

Emma shrugged, "I don't see why not."

"I do."

It was Katie. Her eyes seemed wider than when they'd left and she was chewing on her lip.

"What's wrong?" Regan asked. Katie threw her hands up, surprisingly not losing her balance on Angel.

"What's wrong? What's wrong? Did you see that guy's sword? It was bigger than me! What is a curtain rod going to do against a weapon like that?" she shrieked.

"A tree branch wouldn't be any better," Regan pointed out.

"She's right," Emma said. "And at least the curtain rod will be metal."

"Yeah. Besides, we have the dragons to protect us," Regan reassured. She shared a glance with Rya, smiling. "Everything's going to be fine."

Katie looked momentarily settled. "Maybe you're right."

"Trust me, I am," Regan replied.

The rest of the ride went by smoothly, and by the time they got back, it was almost time for bed. They landed, and Regan was walking to the dome to heat up supper when she remembered something.

"Oh shoot! We were supposed to meet Derrick today!" she exclaimed. Emma started panicking. Rya just laughed.

"Guys, it's fine. Why would he care? We'll just go earlier in the morning and see him. It'll be fine."

Regan was grateful for Rya's calmness. Everyone was so tense in anticipation of the battle, and Rya was so steady and sure that everything would be fine. *Maybe that was why she was so popular back home*, Regan thought.

Officially calmed down, Emma went inside to heat up the chicken. It was the last meal they would get out of the animal, and Regan was glad. Eating the same thing every day made the meal seem bland and boring, when really it was quite delicious. Katie went with her to help.

Regan and Rya hung out with the dragons for a while. The dragons were tired and well fed, having hunted while they were waiting for the girls. Eventually, Nyx settled down for a nap inside the dome next to Nakata, making a roof for the dome with his powers. The roof was pitch black, blocking out any sunlight trying to make its way in. Angel and Ember soon joined them, and the snoring of the four dragons could be heard from miles away.

THE PRIDE

"They really are loud, aren't they?" Rya laughed. Together they walked into the dome. There they found Emma and Katie sitting down at the small table eating. Emma looked guilty when they walked in.

"We didn't know when you were coming in," she said hurriedly.

"Excuses, excuses," Regan chided. She sat down on the ottoman, leaving Rya the last chair. She reached with her fork for the plate of chicken in the middle and grabbed a large piece. After setting it back down on her plate, she dug in.

"Guys," Katie said suddenly, "I don't think Brian is actually bad. I think he just follows Ann."

Regan found herself nodding, "Yeah, I agree."

"Remember, it's Ann and Brian we're talking about here," Emma told them.

"Yeah. But, can anyone be just bad? Or just good?" Rya asked. "Can't you be both?"

"What if Ann and Brian aren't bad, just misled?" Regan said, voicing her thoughts from earlier. "Maybe their ancestors were the ones who were wrong."

"So, you're saying we should give them a chance. After everything they've done? After we figured out what they're planning to do? Are you just going to let them land on Earth, too, then?" Emma asked, clearly upset and doubtful of Regan's ideas.

"No, obviously we're going to stop the rocket." Regan replied. "All I'm saying is that maybe we should, I don't know, let them try to change? Surely they can't be all bad, even if they are evil."

"Maybe," Emma said, still doubtful. Abruptly she stood up, her empty plate held in her hands. "I'm going to go to bed. I'll see you guys in the morning." She threw the plate in the trash and hurried to the bedroom.

"What's her problem?" Rya muttered, taking a bite of the chicken as she did so.

"Cut her some slack. We're all worried about the battle tomorrow," Regan told her friend. She stood up to throw her plate away and, noticing Katie's empty plate, held out her hand for her friend's. With a grateful smile, Katie handed it to her. The plate with the chicken on it was now empty as well, Rya having taken the last of the meat, so Regan picked up that one too. She threw the three plates in the trash and headed for the bedroom, Katie not far behind.

"Hey, wait up," Rya said behind them. Regan turned to see her friend shove the last bites of her chicken into her mouth. After the chicken was gone, Rya stood up so fast that she knocked her chair over, causing a loud thud. With a sheepish grin, she picked the chair back up and hurried to throw her plate away before joining them.

"Graceful," Regan said with a smirk. Rya smiled and did a little hair flip, her short blond hair ending up falling back into her face.

Rya spit out her hair and replied with a laugh, "Thanks."

Laughing, the three girls joined Emma in the bedroom. Each headed to their own separate mattress, and after saying their goodnights, fell asleep to dreams of the upcoming battle.

Chapter 13

The next morning, Regan woke up refreshed. She felt excitement and nervousness at the same time. Today, they would face the Pride, and hopefully, save Earth.

She hurried to get dressed, pulling on a black tank top and bright blue shorts. She tugged on a pair of running shoes and headed to the kitchen. Everyone else was already up and were digging into piles of sausage and eggs. Upon seeing her, Rya waved rapidly. Regan sat down next to Rya and Katie and started eating as well.

"Mmm, these are really good," she said through a mouthful of eggs. "Where'd you get these?"

"Rya got a little too impatient this morning waiting for the dragons to get breakfast, so she went exploring and found a nest of eggs," Emma told her, adding, "Don't worry, there's no baby birds in them." Rya smiled.

"Good, because these are delicious," Regan laughed. They finished the meal quickly, threw away the plates, and walked to a nearby dome to grab curtain rods. After entering the dome and going into the bedroom, they found that the curtain rods were way too high for them to reach standing on the ground.

"Let's stand on the bed," Katie suggested. They did so, and still came up two hands short.

"Here, get on my back," Regan ordered. She climbed onto the bed with Katie. Then her small friend jumped onto Regan's back. Sure, maybe it was dangerous. But they were too excited for the battle to care. Luckily, it worked out, and Katie managed to take the rods off the walls without an accident.

"Ew, these curtains are disgusting!" Rya exclaimed, throwing the curtain onto the ground. The blue and yellow patterned curtains were covered in cobwebs, and spiders scattered across the floor around them.

"Eik!" Katie shrieked as one of the spiders creeped toward her. Emma smashed it with her foot.

"There."

"Thanks," Katie said, wiping her forehead.

"No problem," Emma replied with a smile.

"We need to take the curtains off anyway," Regan said. Rya shook her head.

"I'm not doing it."

"Me neither," said Katie, still eyeing where the spider had been, its body now smushed into the floor.

"Fine, babies, I'll do it," Regan taunted, taking the curtains smoothly off the rod. Dust clouded the air when the fabric dropped onto the ground. Rya glared at her. Katie coughed.

"Well, now that that's done, what next?" Rya asked.

"We should go meet the Pride," Emma replied. "Since we didn't last night."

"Right," said Regan.

"To the dragons we go!" cried Rya, running out the door with the four foot long curtain rod held in her right hand. She accidentally hit the rod against the side of the door, causing her to trip and fall. Regan laughed loudly.

"And that's why you don't rush."

"Shut up." Rya stood up and brushed off her clothes. Walking more slowly this time, Rya headed towards the dragons' nest. The others followed, Katie carrying the other rod as if it were a snake about to bite her.

Soon they arrived at the nest. Rya easily mounted Nakata, still carrying the curtain rod in her right hand while gripping Nakata's neck for balance.

"Why do you still have the rod?" Regan asked.

"Because I'm giving it to Ace," she replied. "It's not like I can just walk into the Pride with a curtain rod in my hand. I was gonna ask him if he could give it to me when we met up with them in the caves."

"I hadn't thought of that." Regan turned to the door, aiming to go and grab the bat and sledgehammer. "Hey, wasn't Emma going to use the curtain rod?"

"Oh, yeah!" Rya tossed the curtain rod down to Emma, who was waiting at Nakata's feet. The metal bar dinged loudly when it fell in front of the pale girl.

"What, you couldn't catch it?" Rya teased. Emma shook her head.

"No, I could've. I just didn't feel like having a metal curtain rod slamming into my palm," Emma fired back. Rya's smile faded.

"Hold on, guys," said Regan. "I'm going to go grab the bat and sledgehammer. Be right back!" Emma nodded, but Regan didn't see it as she ran out of the nest and into the girls' dome. She hurried to the bedroom and grabbed the hammer from where she'd set it against the wall next to her bed. She pulled out her suitcase, as she had when she'd grabbed the sledgehammer, and rifled through it until she found the bright orange aluminum bat. There were a few scuffs on it from previous hits. She stood up, set the hammer down, and took a swing, smiling as she remembered playing with her friends.

"Regan! Hurry up!" Regan heard Katie yell. Quickly, she bent down and grabbed the sledgehammer, almost missing it as she went to sprint out the door. Then, suddenly, she remembered the hearing pills. They'd said they needed them in their plan so they could hear the code word. She'd completely forgotten. She rushed back into her room and grabbed them out of a side pocket in the suitcase. Then she remembered she'd forgotten the phone to watch the recording on as well. Running once again back to her room, she snatched it from where it was sitting on her bed. She put it in her pocket, hoping it wouldn't fall out during the flight.

She ran to the nest, and was breathing heavily once she got there. Everyone else was already mounted on their dragons, and Nyx waited patiently for her to get on his back, his golden eyes shining.

Regan shuffled over to Nakata. She took a deep breath before tossing the bat up to Rya, who fumbled it around a little before managing to catch it.

"Hey, this was my favorite bat!" she exclaimed, turning the orange bat around in her hands.

"Yeah, we know. It was the only one you would use," Regan replied, having finally caught her breath. Emma laughed.

"True fact."

"I grabbed the hearing pills too. I totally forgot we needed them," Regan told them. She stuffed the bottle of pills into one of her pockets.

"Oh yeah!" Emma exclaimed. She must've forgotten too.

"Can we go yet?" Katie asked, shifting on Angel's back. Regan nodded.

"Yeah, let's go."

The dragons took off, roaring gleefully as they rose through the air. Regan just managed to hold onto the sledgehammer while still making sure she didn't fall off. When she looked over to Emma and Katie, she could see they were having even more trouble keeping hold of the curtain rods. In hindsight, they should have tied the weapons onto the dragons, like they had with the containers. But it was too late for that, and they were stuck trying to hang onto the dragons while holding the heavy weapons.

They spotted the volcano that marked the camp's location a short while after having taken off. They landed in the customary clearing, tossing their weapons to the ground before sliding off their dragons.

Regan herself hadn't fumbled the sledgehammer that often, but Rya had had lots of trouble with her bat.

"Phew," Rya wiped beads of sweat from her brow, "that was tough work."

"Sure was," Katie agreed. Picking up their weapons, they headed toward the camp. The dragons knew by now to stay put, so there was no point in telling them to do so.

When Regan had seen the camp for the first time, it had been relatively busy. But that was nothing compared to this. It looked like an ant hill, with people running between houses and towards fire pits. Swords and bows sat on wooden racks, the metal of the swords gleaming in the bright sunlight. Some of the camp members were covered in leather armor from head to two, while others wore only helmets. While they were watching, a young man holding a large wooden club knocked over one of the racks of weapons when he ran past it. The man turned back with a groan and started to pick up the bows, arrows, and swords hurriedly. Katie ran to help him, almost getting trampled on the way. Regan rushed after her, Rya and Emma not far behind her.

"Thank you so much, girls," the man said to them when Katie started picking up the fallen weapons.

"No problem," Katie replied with a smile, "it's really busy today, isn't it?"

"Yeah," laughed the man, "with all the preparations for the battle, this place is a mess."

"We can see that," said Emma, who had knelt down next to Katie and was gathering up the arrows.

"This battle is the biggest thing that's happened around here in a long time," he told them. "Everyone is jumping at the chance for revenge on the Pride."

"I can see why." Regan looked around at everyone. Almost all of them had been a part of the Pride until they were kicked out, save the ones born outside it. She guessed that, in many of their cases, it had been because of the way they looked rather than because of their actions.

"Thank you, ladies," the man said again when they were finished picking up. Emma nodded, and the man ran off again to wherever he had been headed earlier.

"Let's go find Ace and Lucas. Maybe they can tell us where Derrick is," Rya suggested.

"Good idea," Regan replied.

"Over there," said Katie, pointing a little to Regan's left. Regan turned and saw their two friends talking to an older man. Rya shouted Ace's name. The dark-skinned boy glanced around until he finally spotted them. He smiled, waving excitedly. Lucas noticed Ace's movement and eventually found the girls as well. He gestured for them to join them. Emma nodded and led the way towards their friends, weaving through the crowd of people easily. Regan, Katie, and Rya followed close behind her.

"It's safer for you this way," Lucas was saying when they reached them. He was still talking to the old man.

Ace must've seen the confused look on Regan's face because he leaned down slightly and whispered, "He wants to come fight too, but Derrick said that the elders and kids must stay here."

"Oh," Regan paused, "aren't you a kid?"

Ace whisper-laughed, "We just made the cut."

"Awesome," she whispered back with a smile. Then she turned back to the man. Now that she was up close, Regan noticed his snow white hair as well as the many wrinkles in his sunburned skin. He carried a wood cane, and she could tell that he was putting all his weight on it just to be able to stand.

"Please, Lewis, stay here," Lucas was pleading with him. Stubbornly, the man shook his head.

"No, I can fight as well as you can," Lewis said in a shaky voice. Emma strode up to Lucas and tapped his shoulder.

"Let me help," she said quietly. Lucas nodded and stepped aside.

"Don't try telling me I can't go," Lewis said before she could speak. "I can fight."

"I wasn't planning on telling you not to go," Emma said. "I was going to ask if you could stay."

Lewis's eyebrows furrowed, "Ain't that the same thing?"

"No. You see, I was going to ask if you would stay and protect the children."

"Oh."

Emma continued, "What happens if the Pride stages an attack on the camp while we are gone? The kids will need someone to guide them and fight for them."

"Well, I suppose I could stay," Lewis grumbled. "I'll protect those children with my life."

"Thank you," Emma said. With a shaking hand, the old man waved goodbye and hobbled off on his cane, barking orders to the younger men around preparing for the battle. The young men just laughed silently and smiled.

"Thanks, Emma," said Lucas, "without you, I might've been arguing with him forever!"

"Yeah, that was smart thinking," Regan praised. Emma smiled.

"Thanks, guys."

"Hey, that reminds me, Derrick was asking where you guys were yesterday," Ace told them. "You should probably go talk to him."

"Yeah, we were just about to ask you where he was," Rya said. Ace pointed behind where Regan stood to the volcano. A crowd of people surrounded the rock outcropping, and Regan could just make out the figure of Derrick standing on the top of the structure.

"He's over there. We'll come with you," said Ace. Regan nodded, and the group walked together towards Derrick.

"So," Rya asked on the way there, "How are preparations going?"

"Pretty good," Lucas answered. "We had to sharpen a lot of swords yesterday, and they had us making tons of arrows too. Not sure how much help those will be though."

"What do you mean?" Emma asked.

"Well, their base is underground, isn't it? So we can't have any people high up to shoot."

Regan was starting to get confused as well. "Why would they need to be high up to shoot? Doesn't a bow work the same if you're standing on the ground?"

"Archers are near the back of the group," Lucas explained. "If they aren't higher up, they don't have as good of an angle to be shooting. With all of the camp members on the ground in front of them, they could accidentally hit one of our own while aiming for the Pride."

"It's more likely for them to hit camp members than Pride members," Ace simplified.

"Oh," said Rya.

"Maybe Derrick has a plan to solve that problem," Emma said hopefully. Lucas shrugged.

"Maybe."

"Well, we can find out soon enough," Regan pointed out. They'd reached the rock outcropping, and the crowd was just beginning to disperse. Twisting and turning to avoid bumping into anyone, Regan led the way to where she saw Derrick standing at the base of the volcano.

"Sorry we couldn't come yesterday," she said once she finally reached him.

"Yeah, sorry," Emma echoed.

"It is okay, at least you are here now," he gestured to the camp. "I've already set the camp members' preparation jobs and reminded them of the plan."

"Yeah, about the plan. So you know how we said that we didn't know where the rocket was?" Rya prompted. Derrick nodded. "Well, we sort of figured it out."

"How?" he asked incredulously. Regan was confused. Why was it so hard to believe that they figured it out?

"We visited them yesterday so it wouldn't be as suspicious when we saw them today," Katie explained. "They gave us a tour, and they said one of the rooms held a 'special project.'" She then told him where the room was.

"I will inform the members," said Derrick. "You have the pills for the code word, correct?"

Regan pulled out the bottle. "Yeah."

"What is the code word?" Rya asked. "How about panda?"

"Do we even need one?" Katie asked in response. "I mean, won't we be the only ones able to hear it?"

"True," Regan replied. "How about you guys just say when you have everyone out."

"Okay," Derrick agreed. He turned to leave. "See you at the battle."

"Did he even know we were here?" Ace asked when the camp leader was out of earshot.

"I don't think so," Regan admitted.

"Wow," said Lucas. They started walking back towards the camp.

"Okay, I was going to ask you this earlier, but why are you guys carrying curtain rods?" Ace gestured to Emma and Katie.

"They're our weapons," Katie told him.

Ace laughed loudly, "*That* is not a weapon."

"Why not?" Emma asked.

"It just isn't," came the reply. By now they'd reached the camp, and Ace ran to a nearby rack of weapons and selected two short swords. One had a dark grey metal blade with a black leather grip. The other was made of a much lighter metal, this type tinted red. The grip on the second was black leather as well. The second sword's blade was much smaller than the first. Ace ran his eyes over both blades, then ran back to them, the swords held carefully in his hands.

"These are weapons," he said proudly. He handed the smaller sword to Katie, giving the larger and heavier weapon to Emma. Slowly, Katie took the sword, gazing at the blade and biting her lip. Emma, on the other hand, seemed overjoyed. Apparently she didn't like the curtain rod much.

"Thanks, Ace!" Emma exclaimed, turning the sword around in her hands. Ace nodded with a smile.

"My dad made that."

"He did?" Regan asked.

"Yeah, before he got killed by a bison a few years ago." The large boy's head bowed for a moment, then he lifted it back up. Regan didn't think saying anything else would help. The six teens sat in an uncomfortable silence for what seemed like an eternity.

Then, Rya broke it, "Would you guys carry our weapons to the Pride's base?"

"Why can't you bring it?" Lucas asked with contempt.

"Well, we can't just walk in with two swords, a sledgehammer, and a bat and expect to be welcomed," Rya shot back.

Lucas raised his eyebrows and nodded thoughtfully, "Fair point."

"It should be fine," Ace told them. "We can take them now if you want."

Regan nodded and handed her sledgehammer to Lucas, whose arm dropped at the sudden increase of weight. He quickly righted it though, and shot her a grin. Lucas also took Rya's bat. Ace was handed back both of the swords.

"We'll make sure we bring them to the fight," he told them.

"What time is it?" Emma asked. Regan looked at the sun.

"Time for us to get going. It's almost noon," she stated. Lucas nodded.

"We'll tell Derrick you guys are headed over there."

Regan pulled her phone out from her pocket. "Here, take this too. You guys'll need it to watch us on the camera." She showed them how to use the app.

"Okay, thanks," said Lucas. Regan nodded and Rya waved goodbye excitedly.

"See you guys at the battle," Emma said.

Ace smiled. "See you!" he replied. The four of them walked back to the dragons, talking eagerly about the fight.

"I'm gonna be that one person in the movies, you know, the one that does all the cool flips and stuff," Rya was saying.

"Rya, you can't even do a somersault!" Emma exclaimed, laughing. Rya shook her head.

"Can too!"

"Sorry, Rya, but I side with Emma," Katie said. "You really can't."

Rya huffed, "Whatever."

Just then they reached the dragons. As usual, the four dragons were wrestling. Regan had always wondered if the four giant creatures were siblings or not. They'd found them together, but they all looked so different. It was a question that, most likely, would never be answered.

Without the weight of the weapons, getting on Nyx was much simpler for Regan. She easily ran up the big dragon's wing, swinging her left leg around to the other side of Nyx's giant body. Gripping his curled horns, she waited for her friends to mount.

Katie, she noticed, was having more and more trouble getting on Angel. When they'd first tamed the dragons, Katie had struggled because she wasn't strong enough. As the days went on, Katie had gotten stronger and eventually could jump high enough to pull herself the rest of the way. Now, though, it seemed that Katie had to strain to pull herself all the way up.

"Katie, do you need help?" Regan eventually asked. Katie shook her head, sweat beginning to form on her forehead.

"Are you sure?" Emma insisted. "You look like you need help."

"Nope, I got it." Just then Katie launched herself off the ground, grabbing onto Angel's raised spine for purchase. She hauled herself up onto the white dragon's back, flashing a relieved smile at Regan. "See?"

"Alright, let's get going," said Regan. In unison, the four dragons took off, and their final flight before the battle began.

They all agreed that once they caught sight of the Pride's base, they would circle around so it looked like they were coming from the same direction they always did. Regan wasn't sure if the Pride knew of the camp's whereabouts, but it never hurt to be cautious.

Regan daydreamed about the battle as they flew towards their destination. She imagined herself somersaulting and kicking, throwing her adversaries into walls. Then, she realized something, and began berating herself silently. She couldn't just walk in there and start fighting. One reason was because the first part of the plan included the girls distracting Ann and Brian while the Pride got the innocents out. Obviously that wasn't going to work if she just started doing what she'd imagined herself doing. Second, were they really there to fight? The more she thought about it, the more she was convinced they weren't. They'd already asked themselves if Ann and Brian were really to blame for the outcasts. All they'd planned to do was destroy the rocket and secure Ann and Brian. Wouldn't they only be fighting in self-defense, and even then only if the guards decided to defend their leaders?

Maybe she was wrong for doubting her friends and herself. Maybe everything would work out and there would be no fighting. But she couldn't shake that feeling that something was wrong.

"Regan."

The voice snapped Regan out of her thoughts. She glanced around, looking for the source of the sound. It was Rya.

"Regan," she said again, her voice a higher pitch than normal. "We're here."

Indeed, they were. The cave sat below them, and gradually the four dragons lowered themselves to the ground. Only a few people stood outside the cave. Most of them, surprisingly, didn't notice the dragons. The ones who did cast them terrified glances, but didn't move to run or say anything.

Regan slid down Nyx's wing. After she hit the ground, she was almost shoved over by Nyx's enormous head. She held out her hands and hugged his neck. She could feel his hot breath on her back as he wrapped his neck around her, his way of returning the embrace. Backing out of the hug, she took his head in her hands and peered into his golden eyes, his slit pupils staring back at her.

"You can come in if we need help," she told him, "but stay safe."

The dragon gave what seemed like a nod. Satisfied that Nyx understood, she turned and joined her friends where they waited by the entrance to the cave, having already talked to their dragons.

"Ready?" Emma asked. The pale girl fidgeting with her fingers.

"Yep," Regan replied. She handed out the hearing pills, and after everyone had taken one, Emma led the way down into the main cavern. People milled about, talking loudly to one another. Regan picked out Brian's voice among the crowd, and she spotted Brian talking to Wesley across the room. *Head of security*, Regan remembered. Trying to look confident, she strode over to where the two were talking. Rya hastened her step to walk beside her, and Regan shot her a tiny, grateful smile.

Brian noticed the girls when they were still a few steps away from him and Wesley. He waved the big man away and smiled at them.

"Hello!"

"Hi," Regan replied, forcing a smile. Brian gestured for them to follow him and led them down to the left cave, where the office was.

"Welcome back! We'd better get Ann before we show you the gardens. They're amazing," he added. His voice echoed in her ears. The hearing pills had definitely taken effect. They soon reached the office room, and after knocking on the door, Brian opened it to reveal the siblings' office. Everything was still in the same place. The portraits still hung neatly on the walls, the red and gold area rug was still in place, and the bookcase and iguana still sat in the back of the room, along with the stone dragon tucked into the corner where the camera was hidden. Ann was seated in the swivel chair, her feet propped up on the desk. She quickly lowered them when the girls entered. Regan made sure both Ann and Brian's backs were turned before giving the camera a thumbs up. She hoped Lucas and Ace were watching.

"So, should we go see the gardens now?" Brian asked. Regan started to nod, then caught herself. If the gardens were on the opposite side of the network of caves and tunnels, they could miss the signal. They had to be right there in the office, so they could keep the twins away from the action but still hear the camp members from the cafeteria cave.

"Um, can we wait for a little bit?" Regan asked, trying to keep from stuttering, but failing. Emma glanced at her in confusion. "My legs kind of hurt from the ride here, and if it's okay with you, I'd like a rest."

Brian's bewildered look faded. "Oh, yes, of course. I've never really stopped to think about how tired you guys must be. Here, we'll have some lemonade brought up. That should help." He opened the door and leaned out, ringing a small bell on the right side of the wooden door that Regan hadn't noticed before.

Almost instantly a guard appeared at the door. At least, Regan thought it was a guard. He wasn't dressed in the white uniform that Wesley and the other guards wore, but wore a dark red shirt with black slacks. He bowed to Brian, allowing the girls to see his mop of blond hair. He also had a scruffy blond beard and mustache, and his eyes were bright green.

Raising his green eyes, the man asked, "What may I do for you, O High One?"

"Six lemonades, Connor."

"Six lemonades will be here shortly." The man bowed again and left.

"Bring six pillows too!" Brian shouted after him. "For you to sit on," he said to the girls.

"Thanks," said Regan when the lemonade and pillows were brought back.

"It is my pleasure," Connor replied with yet another bow. He returned quickly with six pink lemonades on a silver platter.

"So," Rya started when Connor had left, "what do you guys do all day?"

"What do you mean?" asked Ann, who had so far been quiet.

"Well, you have people to bring you all your drinks and food and stuff. I mean, you're basically royalty! So what do you do all day?" Rya asked again, taking a sip of the pink-colored lemonade. Regan had to admit, Rya was a good distractor.

Brain looked like he was about to answer, then decided against it after seeing a small shake of the head from Ann. "Nothing much."

"So you just sit around all day? Surely you do something fun with your free time," Emma insisted. Brian shrugged.

Ann answered for him, "Sometimes we visit the gardens or the training areas to see how things are going. I like to read the books here though." She pointed to the bookcase. "These, and the stories passed down from our parents, are the only form of entertainment we have really."

"You're joking!" Katie said. "There's no way you haven't read all of those books by now. You must be so bored."

"Yeah, it does get a little boring around here sometimes," Ann admitted. Just then, Regan heard the patter of lots of feet. She glanced at her friends and could tell that they heard it too. The outcasts were here.

Struggling to keep a small smile off her face, Regan tried to continue the conversation. "So, why is the lemonade pink?"

"Is it not supposed to be?" Brian asked.

"On Earth it's a yellow color, unless it's strawberry-flavored," Emma explained.

"I would assume it's because the lemons here are pink," Ann told them. She raised her glass to examine the pink liquid. She swirled it around, the ice clinking in her glass, and took a sip.

"Isn't it hard to make ice here?" Rya asked. Ann shrugged.

"Not especially. I'm not sure how easy it is for you on Earth, but down here in the caves it is cooler than on the surface. We get most of the ice from our deepest caves."

"How deep do the tunnels go?" Katie asked. Regan was actually curious about the question, although she figured Katie had only asked it to further their plan.

"Very deep," Brian replied with a laugh. "It takes ages to walk down there!"

Then, Regan heard the words she'd been waiting for since they'd first heard the outcasts enter.

"This is Lucas. All innocents are out of the caves and are walking back to the camp."

"We're heading for the rocket now," Lucas continued. "Better secure Ann and Brian if you haven't already." A little quieter, they heard him say, "It feels like I'm talking to myself here."

Regan panicked momentarily. How were they supposed to tie Ann and Brian up in their own office? She hadn't thought about that part when they'd originally come up with the plan, and she severely regretted not working it all the way out.

"Hey, can you show me your favorite books? I love to read," said Katie. Ann nodded, and spun in her chair to look at the bookcase thoughtfully. Brian turned his back as well. Regan stared pointedly at Emma, trying to convey her panic and confusion in a single look. Emma must have gotten the message, because she just held up her pointer finger in a clear signal. *Wait.*

Just then, Rya snuck up on Brian and grabbed his hands, the lemonade he'd been holding falling. Rya stuck out her foot to muffle the sound of the glass hitting the floor, the liquid spilling all over her grey tennis shoes. She frowned, but didn't wait long before jumping back into action. She grabbed his hands and pinned them behind his back. Brian tried to speak, but his mouth was quickly covered by one of Rya's hands. Emma pulled out a thin, but strong looking vine from the back pocket of her jean shorts. Swiftly, but silently, she wrapped the vine around his hands, still held firmly behind his back. Apparently, Brian was really weak, as Rya only had to keep one hand clamped around his wrists to keep them put.

The finished product was Brian with his hands securely tied behind his back, Rya's hand still held over his mouth to prevent any noise. Rya looked at Regan and jerked her head towards Brian. Regan understood and quickly moved to put her hand over Brian's mouth in place of Rya's. But, during the switch, Brian managed to get out one word.

"Ann!"

Ann turned around in a flash. As soon as she saw the scene, Regan with her hand slammed back over Brian's mouth, Rya standing next to her with her hands held in the air in surrender, and Emma behind the three with her hands holding Brian's wrists, her eyes narrowed.

"I *knew* you were trouble!" she exclaimed. She moved to launch herself at Rya, who still stood uncertainly next to Brian, but the red-haired girl fell to the floor before she even got out of the chair.

Katie, who had gone with Ann to the bookcase, had tackled her from behind. She now lay sprawled on Ann's back, her skinny forearms pressing against Ann with all her might. It was a losing fight. But luckily, Katie had backup. Regan rushed over and pushed down on Ann's legs. Katie shifted her weight to Ann's arms, and together the two girls pinned down the girl. Her green eyes gleamed wildly when she turned to look up at them.

"You're going to regret this," Ann hissed at them. Emma came over with another vine and tied Ann's hands behind her back as well.

"It's not our fault we had to tie you up. You were the ones building a rocket to take over Earth!" Katie exclaimed.

Ann's eyes widened, "How'd you find out about that?!"

Smugly, Regan walked over to the dragon statue in the corner and plucked up the camera from where she had left it. "This is how."

"You little. . ." she trailed off. Then, a vicious smile broke out on her face. "How do you expect to beat us? You're only four girls. Do you know how many guards we have?"

"Nope, and we don't care how many you have," said Regan. She didn't say anything else. She almost felt like one of the supervillains in the movies she watched, and once again she wondered if they were doing the right thing.

It was too late now though. They'd secured Ann and Brian. All that was left was the final step. *Destroy the rocket.*

Quickly, they tied thicker strands of vine around the siblings' mouths. Then, they ran out of the room, rushing to the room they'd been told held the special project. But upon entering the room, they didn't find just the rocket.

The giant rocket sat in the back of the room, towering over them. A few of the panels on the outside of it were still missing, but it was otherwise finished. Lucas and Ace were tied up in chains in the middle of the room, multiple other outcasts were also trapped on the outskirts of the room. Lucas tried to mumble something, but his mouth was covered in tape. Then, Derrick stepped out from the shadows behind the rocket. He wore the same flowing robes they'd seen him in the first time they'd met him, and his blue eyes gleamed.

"Hello ladies," he said in his usual greeting. This time though, it sounded much more sinister.

"What are you doing?!" Rya exclaimed, glancing from their two friends, then to the outcasts around the room, her eyes finally resting again on Lucas and Ace. Lucas's eyes were wide, but Ace was slumped forward, his eyes closed. Derrick smiled.

"Didn't you ever wonder how I came to be leader of the camp?" he asked, laughing. "It was all because of Ann and Brian."

Regan was speechless. Derrick continued, "You see, when the rules for the Pride were first established, anyone who broke the rules was killed. But, when Ann and Brian inherited the leadership, they didn't have the heart to kill the offenders. So they came to me." He paused, his head lifted to the ceiling, and sighed, "Oh, I remember that day. The twins wanted to banish the rule breakers instead of killing them. They asked me to take care of the offenders and lead them. Obviously, I agreed."

"That's when the camp started. Our system worked so well. But, it wasn't enough." He circled the two boys like a shark circling around its prey. "I'd always wanted to be a leader. A king. At first, the outcasts saw me as their savior. The camp was their refuge. Eventually, the people stopped thanking me and worshipping me, rather, they took the camp for granted! Imagine that!" He laughed. Regan could only stand and watch as he continued to circle her friends, scared of what he would do if she made a move towards them. Emma, Katie, and Rya were frozen in place as well.

"So, I took things into my own hands. I arranged a visit with Ann and Brian to 'tell them how things were going'. But I did a little bit more on my visit." He smiled again. He paused in his steps to stare at the four girls. "The guards were getting tired of Ann and Brian's constant demands. More this, more that. So, I invited them to my cause. Help me, I told them, and you won't have to worry about Ann and Brian's thirst and hunger anymore. They eagerly took my offer."

Lucas tried once again to speak, but the sound still came out muffled and Regan couldn't understand the words. Derrick smacked him hard on the back of the head.

"Quiet, boy!"

He smiled again. "As I was saying, the guards work for me now. You've already taken care of Ann and Brian for me. Thank you, by the way." He finished, his voice thick with glee, "Now all I have to do is take care of you."

Then Regan felt something slam into the back of her head, and everything went dark.

Chapter 14

Regan woke up in a dark room. The back of her head ached painfully, and she could barely see where she was. The only light came from a small candle set on a plate in the center of the room. Her other three friends were lying around the candle, and slowly each girl got up. Regan rubbed her head to try and get rid of the pain, but to no avail.

"Where are we?" asked Rya, who was also rubbing her head. Regan pushed herself to a sitting position with her hands.

"I have no clue, but we have to get out and save Lucas and Ace!" She didn't even want to think of what might've already happened to them.

"How?" asked Emma. "We don't even know where the door is, let alone how to get back to that room!"

Katie started to cry, "What have we done?"

"Oh, Katie." Regan crawled over to her friend and hugged her tightly. "We're gonna fix this."

"How?" Always that question of how. This time, Regan had an answer. She picked up the candle and showed it around the room, lighting up every dark corner until she found a large metal dark. She carried the candle with her and saw the round metal handle. She didn't expect it to open, but she tried anyway. Locked.

"Okay." As usual, she was prepared. Back home on earth, she'd sewed a lock pick into the pair of shoes she was wearing now. At the time it had been for fun, more so she could be like the heroes in the movies than for actual use. But she had taught herself to use it, and she pulled it out of her shoe with a grim smile. She easily picked the lock and the door swung outward. Regan shone the candle outside to reveal a dirt tunnel that sloped steeply upwards.

"Awesome! We're free!" Rya exclaimed happily, standing up to join Regan near the door.

"Can't be this simple, can it?" Regan asked herself. She walked out to the tunnel and led her friends to the top. The others trusted her completely to lead them out of the mess they'd led themselves into.

At the top of the hill was another wooden door. This one wasn't locked, however, and it opened silently to the main cavern. When she realized where the door opened, Regan quickly snuffed out the candle. Regan was surprised he hadn't sent any guards to watch them. Derrick had extremely underestimated them when he'd sent them down to that room.

But they weren't clear yet. They were lucky Regan had extinguished the light, because multiple guards patrolled the cavern. Every single one of them was twice their size and covered in muscle. Their only chance was stealth.

"Alright," Regan whispered, barely mouthing the word. She knew they could hear her still because of the pills they'd taken. "We're going to sneak outside and grab Angel. She can help us take out the guards in here." She saw a question rising to Rya's lips and hurried to answer it before her friend's loud whisper gave them away.

"The others are too big to fit in here without collapsing the entrance. We'll have to lead everyone outside for the actual battle. As soon as we get past the guards in here, we'll lead Angel to the rocket room. You guys'll free the others. Once the outcasts are free, you guys have to go to the training room. See if you can find any weapons we can use. Then get outside."

"What about you?" Emma mouthed. Regan shook her head, the movement hard to see in the darkness.

"I need to distract Derrick. Without him it should be easier to beat the guards."

"But he's stronger than you!" Katie whispered forcefully.

Regan shushed her, "I know, but I'm not going to face him head on. I'll lead him away from you guys, then as soon as I know you're all out, I'm going to join you."

"What about Ann and Brian?" Rya asked. "We can't just leave them here."

"Free them when you leave. Make sure you tell them about Derrick before untying them though. We don't want them turning on us after what happened."

"Okay," Emma agreed, "I still don't like leaving you though."

"You don't have to like it." Regan cracked the door open a little farther. "Everyone ready?"

"Yeah," came the reply. Slowly, Regan pushed open the door, making sure not to make any noise. Once it was open far enough, she stepped out. Grabbing Emma's arm behind her, she gently pulled her friend out as well. Emma, in turn, grabbed Rya, and Rya grabbed Katie to form a chain. Regan shuffled away from the door, keeping along the wall of the cave.

The sounds of their steps echoed in Regan's ears, and she prayed it was because of the hearing pills. Rya stepped on a pebble, and it scattered across the ground. To Regan, it sounded like a boulder rolling down a mountain.

One of the guards paused. In the darkness, he turned toward them. He carried a torch and shone it in front of him.

"Who's there?" he demanded. Regan held her breath, tightening her hold around Emma's arm.

When no other sound presented itself, the man grunted and turned away from them. "Probably a rat."

Regan slowly let out the breath she'd been holding. *Phew, that was close.*

She kept inching her way to the cavern entrance, every now and then pausing for a guard to go by. Without further incident, they made it to the entrance. Luckily the sun had set, and it was just as dark outside as it had been in the cave. No guards were stationed by the opening, and Regan had to force herself to resist the urge to run out of the cave.

Once they reached the top, they found the four dragons tied to the ground with giant chains that wrapped around their scaled bodies. Ember's were glowing red hot, and a few of his chain links had dropped to the ground in piles of melted metal. If he'd been left a little longer, he probably would have escaped on his own. Angel had a good chance of doing so as well, her ice powers causing the metal to turn brittle and break. Many of her chains also lay on the ground.

Nakata and Nyx were struggling though. Nyx was sprawled on his side and had ropes of dark clouds wrapped around him in addition to the chains, and it looked like the clouds were trying to rip the chains off him. But because the clouds weren't fully solid, his attempts had no effect. Nakata's vines were the same, trying to weave in and out through the chain links but in reality only making her more tangled.

"Oh, Nyx." Regan rushed to the dragon's side, taking out the lock pick again. She found the lock and quickly undid it, the chains falling limply off him. Nyx stood and shook them off, the metal piling around him. He nudged her once with his head to indicate his gratefulness, then jerked his head toward Nakata. Regan wondered how Derrick and his minions had even managed to get the chains on the dragons.

After undoing the lock on Nakata, Regan gathered her friends together. All of them had been talking to their dragons gently. The dragons formed a circle around the four girls when they finally met up again, making a wall between them and the cave.

"Does Angel know she's coming with us?" Regan asked. Katie nodded.

"Yeah."

"Everyone ready to go?" Regan checked again. More yeses. "Alright, let's do this."

They didn't sneak back in, Angel being too big to go unseen. So, instead, they decided to run in. Angel went first, her body being more protected from the guards' weapons.

As soon as the guards caught sight of the white dragon, their eyes widened. They charged at Angel, their spears, clubs, and swords held before them. But Angel's frosty breath stopped them in their tracks, the men frozen in place, literally. Their weapons were covered in a solid layer of ice as well. There was no way they were going to cause the girls any problems.

When all the guards were encased in ice, Angel turned back to look at them. She'd frozen the torches as well, and now the only light came from the cafeteria where they were headed.

Regan went first this time, the others stayed back so that, when Regan led Derrick away from the rocket room, they could rush in and save their friends. She walked cautiously, peeking around the corner to check if there were any guards. There were two stationed next to the door, multiple others patrolling around the room. Derrick stood in conversation with one in the middle of the cafeteria. All the tables sat empty, the only thing on them was the food the Pride members had left when they'd ran to the safety of the camp.

Regan stepped out from the shelter of the wall and into full view of the guards. The one talking to Derrick noticed her first, and he pointed at her.

"Sir, she's escaped!"

Derrick's eyes narrowed and he turned on the guard, slapping him on the arm. "Well, don't tell me about it! Go get her!"

The guard frowned, but obediently started running towards Regan, a few others following him.

"What, Derrick, can't catch me yourself?" Regan taunted. She was walking dangerously. She had nothing to defend herself with, her only weapon, her words.

"Oh, you little maggot!" Derrick grabbed a wooden club from the nearest guard and charged Regan. "Get the other three girls, this one is all mine."

"Pfft, yeah right. Like your skinny arms could hurt me," she replied with a laugh as she dodged his first attack. The club smashed into the stone. Derrick roared with anger and charged again. This time the weapon barely missed her, Regan spinning at the last second to avoid being smashed.

The club ended up getting stuck in the rock for a second, and while Derrick was distracted trying to yank it back out, Regan ran into the tunnel leading to the bedrooms and training areas. She passed a few guards as she ran, all of them staring after her with confused looks. Apparently the Pride members selected as guards weren't very bright.

After a little while of running, Regan stopped and caught her breath outside one of the many classrooms. She looked back to where she had come and saw Derrick shoving his way through guards, his red robes billowing behind him. Hatred was clearly evident on his face. He still held the club, but now a large crack ran through the head of it. She tried to look behind him for any sign of Angel and her friends, but found none.

Regan ducked into the classroom and closed the door forcefully behind her. The room was full of wooden desks and red plastic chairs. A chalkboard was hung on one wall. Cups full of pens and pencils sat on the large desk at the front of the room, presumably where the teacher sat. She scanned the room for a place to hide. It had to be somewhere that Derrick couldn't see her easily, but in a spot where she could still run away if needed.

Finally, she spotted a place in the far back corner from where she stood. It was a small reading area set deeper into the ground. The dip in the ground was flush with the wall and was separated from the rest of the room by a small, empty bookcase. She ran to the hollow and crouched down behind the bookcase, her head sticking out on one side so she could see the door.

She was just in time. As soon as she was hidden from view, the door opened, and Derrick walked in. She pulled her head farther back behind the bookcase. Now that the camp leader was closer, she could see that his club was really cracked. One more hit and it would shatter. He must've hit the ground really hard. *That could've been me,* Regan thought.

"Come out, come out, wherever you are," Derrick called with a laugh. "Playing hide and seek now are we?"

He crept closer, but it didn't look like he'd spotted her yet. As she watched, he checked behind the teacher's desk and around all the students' desks as well. Soon, he caught sight of the reading area, and he smiled. Once again, Regan found herself comparing it to that of a shark's.

Slowly, he approached the bookcase. "You know, it really is a shame. I could've found a good use for you. I was impressed with your planning skills. You could've been, perhaps, my strategist. Although I guess it's too late for that now, isn't it?" He was right in front of the bookcase. He peered over the top of it, smiling again when he saw her crouched there. Then he swung.

Regan rolled to the left as soon as she saw his arm move. The club hit the ground where she'd been lying only a second ago. Upon impact both the club and the bookcase splintered and broke, wood flying everywhere. Regan pushed herself to her feet and darted toward the teacher's desk. Getting an idea, she grabbed the cup of pencils and pens and spun around. Derrick, she saw, had fallen forward when he'd broken the bookcase, and he was now standing up slowly. His robes were torn in some places, the blood red fabric hanging from his arms in thin strips. He turned to face her, his eyes glittering with increased anger.

"Didn't like that, huh?" Regan asked, a smirk playing on her face. It was all an act though. Inside, she was terrified. Derrick was so much bigger than her, and he was more experienced too.

"Shut up you little brat!" he screeched. Without his club, he was at less of an advantage than he had been earlier, which was good. But he was still very much a threat.

"Sure, as soon as you stop chasing me," she replied. With another growl of anger he rushed at her. Regan grabbed one of the pencils and threw it at him like a dart. She was really good at throwing darts, and she hoped throwing a pencil would be similar. She aimed for his face, but it hit Derrick in the chest instead. He flinched, but otherwise the pencil didn't seem to bother him.

By now he was almost on her, and in a split second decision she threw the whole cup of writing utensils at him. Out of pure luck, the cup struck him in the face, all the pens and pencils scattering around his feet. In his moment of distraction, Regan rushed out of the classroom, firmly slamming the door behind her.

Whereas the tunnel before had been filled with a couple guards every few yards, now there was nobody. She ran with all her speed back towards the cafeteria, where she could hear the sounds of fighting.

When she was about halfway there she heard the door open and close behind her, along with the pounding of feet. She turned to see Derrick rushing after her.

"You're going to regret that!" he yelled.

"Doubt it," Regan yelled back in false confidence. She reached the cafeteria with her breath coming in ragged gasps, her chest aching for lack of oxygen. She paused momentarily to breathe and looked around the room.

Guards encased in thick ice were leaned against the tables or standing on their own throughout the room. Many of the frozen security guards wore scared expressions on their faces. The sounds of fighting she'd heard earlier came from the outcasts and the guards engaged in battle. She looked around for her friends, and soon saw all three of them teaming up on Wesley. His white uniform was stained with dirt and sweat covered his skin. The three girls were giving him quite a hard time. While she was watching, Emma darted in with her sword, smacking Wesley's side with the flat of the blade. When the big man turned to confront her, Rya hit him from behind with her bat. A thud thundered in Regan's ears, the effects of the still not completely worn off. Wesley crumpled to the ground, his brown eyes closed. Rya had knocked him out! Rya and Katie exchanged a high five, then quickly returned to the fight.

The sound of running footsteps grew louder, and Regan turned to see Derrick almost on her. With renewed energy Regan sprinted across the room, leading Derrick through the crowd. She wove between the fighting people, outcasts and guards battling each other viciously. The sound of swords clashing against each other rang around the room. Once Regan reached the other side of the room, she turned around.

Only to find a hand clamped around her throat.

"Gotcha!" Derrick laughed. "Did you really think you could outrun me forever? None of this battle will matter. The security guards will demolish your little friends, and then I'll be king."

"Is this what you call demolishing?" Regan choked out. Derrick's grip tightened.

"You dare speak against me when I hold your life in my hands."

She couldn't reply this time. She was struggling just to breathe. Nobody noticed the two people, everyone caught up in their own battles. She kicked at Derrick's legs, trying to free herself from his strong hold.

"There's no escape," Derrick told her. He lifted her off the ground so they were level, eye to eye. Feebly, she tried kicking again, but didn't connect with anything. She scratched at his hands, fighting for air. Derrick's blue eyes were cold, no ounce of mercy visible.

"Was it really worth it?" he asked her. Regan closed her eyes and waited for unconsciousness.

But it never came. She heard a thunk, and the pressure from her throat was released. She collapsed to the ground, gasping for air. She opened her eyes to see Lucas holding her sledgehammer. The boy knelt next to her.

"Are you okay?" he asked, his voice thick with worry.

"Yeah, thanks to you," she coughed. She glanced down at Derrick, his eyes closed. He looked almost peaceful, a sharp contrast to his anger a few moments ago. Lucas stood and held out a hand to help her up. Gratefully, she took it.

"Where's Ace?"

"Over there," Lucas pointed to the left of them, where Ace was battling a large-blond haired man in a white uniform. The two traded swings with each other, Ace using a longsword and the guard using a metal staff.

"Let's go help him!" Regan moved to run, but Lucas stopped her with a hand.

"He's got it. Besides, you've done your part. Now let us do ours," he said to her. Then he left, Rya coming over to take his place. The girl's short blond hair was stuck to her forehead with sweat. She didn't seem to be injured.

"Regan! You're all right!" Rya hugged her, then pulled back to examine her. "What happened to your neck?"

"I'll tell you later. What happened to moving the fight outside?" Regan asked. She put her hand on the wall for balance.

"Uh," Rya scratched the back of her head with her right hand, the bat held in her left. "qe forgot about that part?"

"We still have time," Regan said. Louder, she shouted, "Lead them outside!"

Ace heard it first. He struck one last time, hard, at his opponent with the flat of his blade, leaving him reeling. Then he turned and sprinted outside. A few others noticed and followed his lead, striking the guards they were fighting as hard as they could and then turning on their heels and running to the cave's entrance. Soon, all the outcasts were heading towards the entrance. Katie was near the front with Ace and Emma brought up the back. She gave Regan an encouraging thumbs up before running out of the cafeteria. Rya and Regan ran after her.

"Where's Angel?" Regan asked when they were almost to the top. She was struggling again to breathe, a combination of her recent choking and all the running she'd been doing.

"We made her go back outside once we freed the camp members. It would've been too risky to keep her with us. She could've frozen some of our own," Rya told her. Regan nodded.

"Smart decision. Did you free Ann and Brian too?"

"Yeah," Rya answered, drawing out the word. "They weren't too happy to see us at first, but after we explained what happened they let us help them." Just then they reached the top of the uphill climb, and walked outside.

The four dragons stood in a semi-circle facing the entrance, their legs braced like something was about to slam into them. All four heads were lowered to the ground, their mouths open in silent growls. All the outcasts had gathered behind the four beasts, and Regan saw Lucas, Ace, and Katie standing behind Nyx's spiked tail. Regan ran to join them, Rya close behind her. Emma was there too.

"Is everyone okay?" Regan asked when she reached her friends.

"We should be asking you that," Katie replied. "You were the one facing Derrick all by yourself."

"I'm fine, thanks to Lucas," Regan replied, shooting him another grateful glance.

He smiled, "That sledgehammer sure is handy."

"You only knocked Derrick out, right?" Regan asked, suddenly worried they'd killed someone.

Lucas nodded, "I think so. I didn't hit him very hard."

"Where are Ann and Brian?" Regan then asked.

"Right here," said Ann's voice. Regan turned around to see the siblings standing right behind her. Ann looked slightly mad, but Brian was more shocked than angry. Regan thought she understood. Derrick had probably known them their entire lives, and they probably thought of him as a trustworthy friend, maybe even something like family.

"You're not too mad at us, are you?" Regan asked hopefully.

"No," Ann admitted. "I get why you did it."

"Is everyone out?" Emma checked. A young woman just running out of the cave answered her.

"Yes. I was the last one out."

"Alright dragons, do your stuff," said Rya. No sooner had she said it than the remaining guards ran out of the cavern, their weapons held in front of them, ready to strike.

Ember blew a wave of flame their way, not close enough to set them on fire, but just close enough to singe their clothes and their hair. The guards stumbled back. Next, Angel tried. Her powers were weaker, though, from having used them so much, and all she got out was a thin stream of frost.

Third came Nyx and Nakata. Nyx did something Regan had never seen him do before. Usually he used his power to make darkness, but as Ann and Brian had once told them, he could also control light. He did so now, making a bright flash that blinded the guards. While the men were blinded and disoriented, Nakata stomped her feet, making vines that rose up out of the ground and tangled around the security guards' feet. All the men fell, and Nakata made it even harder for them to rise when she continued making vines that swirled around the men's bodies, trapping them against the ground.

Cheers of triumph went out among the crowd.

"We aren't done yet," Ace said. "We still haven't destroyed the rocket, and Derrick is still down there."

"I thought we agreed to destroy the rocket while you were freeing people!" said Regan.

"We were too occupied with the guards. Besides, Angel's power only lasted so long. She hasn't had enough practice with it. We thought she should rest, and then we could try again later when all the guards were taken care of," Emma explained.

Regan leaned forward before whispering, "But will Ann and Brian let us destroy the rocket?"

"I guess we'll see," Emma replied. After making sure that the guards truly weren't going anywhere, the six friends ran back into the cave. Lucas and Ace went first, the sledgehammer and sword better defenses than the rest of their weapons.

They found Derrick first, tying his hands behind his back with a vine, like they'd done with Ann and Brian. They tied his feet together too, and they propped him up against the wall in a seated position. He was still unconscious. Once again, Regan wondered if they'd killed him. She didn't let herself dwell on the thought for long though.

"That should do it," Rya said, stepping back to admire her handiwork. Derrick was securely tied up, and there was no way he was going anywhere.

"Alright, let's go see about this rocket," Regan replied. She didn't bother about being quiet, as she doubted there were any guards left to attack them.

She was wrong about that. As soon as they opened the door to the rocket room, two people rushed out at them. One was slender, with green eyes, a mop of blond hair, and a bushy beard. The other was slightly taller and broader, with a red mullet. Both carried wooden clubs.

Regan confronted the first, giving him a hard kick to the stomach that sent him keeling. Lucas and Ace took on the second. Dropping their weapons, they each went on different sides of the man. Emma quickly picked up Ace's sword and blocked the man's first swing at Ace. Ace punched the guard in the gut. When the guard stepped back to get away from Ace, he ran into Lucas, who promptly shoved him back towards Ace. The big, dark-skinned boy landed another hard hit to the face and the guard dropped.

The smaller guard hadn't given up yet though. After recovering from Regan's first kick, he stood up and lunged at Katie. He was stopped a few feet short by a sweeping kick to the guard's feet by Rya, causing the man to fall to the ground with a loud thud. He dropped his club in the process, and as he reached for it, Regan kicked it across the room. Then Lucas and Ace held down his arms while Rya and Emma held his legs.

"Here, Katie!" Emma said, holding the man's leg with one hand while she grabbed two more vines out of her pocket and tossed it to the small girl. Katie caught it with ease and handed one of them to Regan. Regan tied the man's hands together, while Katie tied his feet. Rya tied up the other guy too, but no one needed to hold him down while she did so.

When they were done, they dragged the two men over to the wall and laid them there. The whole time they were tying and dragging the small guard was yelling at them, screaming about how they'd regret the things they did.

"Derrick will defeat you!" the man shouted at one point, clearly believing in his new leader.

"Actually, he won't, because he is currently just as unconscious and tied up as your friend there," Lucas told the man, pointing to the larger guard. The smaller guard scowled, and it was only then that Regan recognized him. It was Connor, the man who'd brought them the lemonades. She remembered him bowing to Ann and Brian. She actually felt bad for the siblings. The guards' false loyalty must've been a huge blow.

"Will he never shut up?" Ace asked after a few more minutes of angry rambling. Emma shrugged, then, without warning, she darted out of the room. Regan and Katie shared a confused look until Emma reappeared holding a thicker vine. This one was also flatter than the others, and Emma went over to Connor and tied it around his mouth. He tried to yell again, but this time all that came out was a muffled sound. He tried a couple more times, then gave up, slouching against the wall.

"Good idea!" Katie exclaimed.

"We're getting pretty good at this," Rya remarked.

"At beating people up or tying them up?" Regan asked with a slight laugh.

Rya gave a one shoulder shrug, "Both, I guess."

They continued walking until they were close enough to touch the rocket. A few of the metal panels were missing from the exterior of it, allowing the six friends to see inside to the metal framework.

"So... how are we going to destroy this thing?" Lucas asked, carefully examining the rocket.

"I have no clue," Regan replied. She stared up at the top of the rocket. It reminded her of a kid's drawing of a rocket ship, with the red cone and fins, the circular window, and the silver metal panels. "Can they even use this thing?"

"I mean, I'm no NASA scientist or anything, but to me it looks like it's stuck here," said Katie.

"But if there even is a chance it could fly..." Emma started.

"We have to destroy it," Lucas finished.

"Hold on," Regan interrupted. "What if Ann and Brian don't want to take over Earth anymore? What if they've changed, or something?"

"Regan, think how long this would've taken to build. Do you really think that, after all that hard work, they're just going to say 'I don't want to go to Earth anymore,'" Emma pointed out. "Not likely."

"True."

"Do you think Angel could do it?" Katie asked. "You saw what was happening with the chains. What if she could get the metal cold enough to break?"

"Ember could probably melt it," Emma added.

"Yeah, both sound ideas, except for the fact that Angel is extremely weak and tired right now, and Ember is too big to fit even his head through the doorway." Regan said.

"We could just smash it," Lucas offered, lifting up his sledgehammer.

"Yeah, but that would take *forever*," Rya complained. "I don't think I have that kind of patience."

"Do you think there's some way we could, I don't know, deactivate it?" Ace asked.

"It isn't a bomb," Emma replied sharply.

"Just a suggestion," Ace said, throwing his hands in the air in mock surrender.

"Why don't we work on getting all the tied up and frozen people outside. Then we have time to think on it a little, and hopefully by then Angel will be rested enough to help," Regan said.

Lucas nodded, "Good idea."

Regan and Rya carried Connor out, Regan holding his legs and Rya holding his arms. He thrashed around at first, but eventually laid still. He was fairly light, and the two girls barely had any trouble getting him out of the cave.

The other guard was a whole different matter. It took the other four people just to lift him up, one on each limb. Even then they had trouble, and Regan and Rya had to rush back in to help. All six of them managed to carry him out of the cavern, but only with a lot of struggling. They repeated the process with Derrick, who was still unconscious. Once the people outside saw what they were doing, they pitched in to help. Eventually they had a steady stream of people carrying guards trapped with ice out of the cave. They laid all the guards down nicely a few yards away from the entrance, trusting the dragons to watch them.

Regan and her friends were just beginning to lift up another guard when Regan heard a low rumbling sound.

"You guys hear that?" she asked, receiving nods in return. The effects of the healing pills must've worn off, because the boys could hear the noise as well. They paused, waiting to hear the sound again.

The next time they heard it, a few chunks of dirt and stone fell from the ceiling. Regan saw Emma duck to avoid being hit.

"Let's keep moving," Lucas suggested, also having noticed Emma's close call. They proceeded to walk slowly, dodging the occasional dirt clod or rock with ease. Again they heard the rumbling noise, and this time even more dirt and stone fell. By now the other people in the cave had noticed, and they started moving faster toward the exit.

"What's happening?" asked Katie. Then came a loud boom, and the ceiling near the center of the cave started to collapse. There was one group of people that had been walking under the area, and panic broke out. The group started running towards the exit, causing other people to sprint as well.

"Earthquake!" someone shouted. Regan and Rya glanced at each other, the alarm evident in their expressions. Instantly they started sprinting to the entrance of the cave. They barely made it out before the cave truly started to crumble apart. Regan glanced back to make sure no one else was behind them, and it was her last look at the Pride's home before it collapsed in a shower of dirt and rock. The few stalactites that hung from the ceiling fell and shattered on the ground, scattering shards of rock everywhere. A cloud of dust rose from the ground, and once it cleared, the Pride's cavern was nothing more than a hole in the ground. All that was left of the Pride's home was the bright red nose cone of a rocket, sticking up just slightly from where the dust and dirt had settled.

Slowly, they lowered the guard they carried to the ground. Regan looked around at her friends and saw sad, sorry faces. That was not how they'd planned to get rid of the rocket.

Regan heard crying behind her, and turned to see Ann and Brian hugging each other tightly, their heads buried into one another's shoulders. Regan felt terrible for them. Maybe all the fighting had caused the earthquake. Maybe it was all the noise they'd made, or maybe it was their fault at all. Maybe it had been bound to happen.

Either way, the Pride's home was gone.

She approached the two siblings carefully, her friends behind her. "I am so sorry."

Ann turned to her and wiped away a tear. "What are we going to do? This is the only home we've ever known!"

Regan paused for a moment. She honestly had no idea. She doubted the camp members would let them back in, even after they found out about Derrick.

Then Katie spoke up, "What if they come live with us?"

Rya looked confused, "Huh?"

"What if they come live with us?" Katie said again. "We have enough domes for everyone. The outcasts could come too!"

"You know, that's actually a pretty good idea," Regan agreed.

"You'd let us do that?" Brian asked, tears still streaming down his face.

"Yeah! Why not?" Rya asked.

"Why not?" Emma forcefully whispered to her friends. "Why not? Did you forget that these guys have been building a rocket to take over Earth?"

"I think they'll turn out to be alright," Regan replied quietly. "They don't have servants anymore and their rocket is buried. Besides, who's going to help them build another one?"

"She has a good point," Rya said.

Emma hesitated.

"C'mon, Emma," Katie pleaded. She sounded like a child begging their parents for a pet.

"Alright fine," Emma conceded.

A smile broke out on Katie's face, "Yes!" the small girl exclaimed with a fist pump. She immediately went over to Ann, put an arm around the girl, and started telling her about all the cool things they would do. Regan couldn't remember the last time she'd seen Katie this excited. Ann turned back and mouthed *thank you*. Regan smiled and nodded.

"Thanks guys," Brian said, wiping his eyes again. He smiled weakly. "Maybe we'll turn out to be pretty good friends." Then he walked off to join Katie and his sister.

Regan turned to the rest of her friends and smiled. Despite the Pride's home collapsing, they'd won.

"Let's go home," said Rya.

Chapter 15

During the aftermath of the battle, everyone was pitching in to help move Ann and Brian, as well as the outcasts, into their new homes. They dedicated one dome to holding Derrick and the guards, all of which had been thawed and tied up. It would serve as a sort of prison, until they voted to release them. Regan figured it would be a while until Derrick was free again.

Lucas's family moved into the dome to the left of the girls', and Ace and his mom moved to the dome directly to the right. The six friends made sure everyone knew not to go into their fort dome, and the smaller families donated mattresses to the people who chose domes that had been emptied of them earlier, either from when the girls had made the dragons' nest or when they'd made their fort.

Regan was happy. All her friends were in one place, Earth was no longer in danger, she had Nyx, and all was well. The only thing she still wished for was her family.

And two days after the battle, she got her wish.

Chapter 16

The four girls were hanging out with the dragons when it happened. It had been a relatively busy few days, with everyone moving in, and Regan was happy to have a day to rest. She was lounging comfortably against Nyx's side when the dragon picked his head up from where it lay on the ground, turning it up to the sky.

"What is it, Nyx?" Regan asked. Nyx snorted. Nakata, Ember, and Angel were all looking at the red sky as well. Regan glanced at Rya. Her friend's face was confused at first, but then turned to a look of utter shock and joy.

"Regan, look!" Rya shouted, pointing up at the sky. Finally, Regan glanced up. A sleek NASA rocket was headed for the area right outside the dome town. Regan jumped to her feet and sprinted as fast as she could to the landing site, making sure not to get too close, lest she get injured. She glanced back to see her three friends laughing with glee behind her, while the dragons just laid there. They had no idea what was happening, how big of a deal this was to the girls.

Once the rocket safely landed, the door opened, and out emerged all four of the girls' families. Regan's mom and dad were first out of the rocket, her two sisters after them. Her mother took her first steps on Vulcan, and upon seeing Regan, threw off her space helmet and ran towards her. Her mother's thick, blond hair flew behind her as she sprinted for her daughter. Regan embraced her mom in a tight hug, burying her head in her shoulder. At once all her homesickness vanished. Her dad and sisters joined in on the hug, and soon everyone was crying of joy. Regan remembered just how much she had missed her family, and she was so grateful they'd been able to finally make it to the planet.

"Oh, honey," said Regan's mom in her soft, gentle voice, "we missed you so much."

"I missed you, too," Regan replied, hugging her family even tighter. She laughed. "What took you guys so long?"

Her mom replied, "The transportation system took longer than they expected to finish." Regan nodded, and the five descended into a comfortable moment of silence as they hung onto each other.

Eventually, Regan's dad broke the hug.

"So, what have you been doing all this time?" he asked in his familiar, deep voice.

"Yeah, Regan, tell us!" Audrey exclaimed, her black hair in pigtails. Liza's blond hair sported the same style. Regan stared into their bright green eyes, smiled, and glanced to where her friends were also hugging their families. She caught Emma's eye, who returned the look with a smile.

"It's a long story."

So the four girls brought their families together in the building that had become their home, and told the stories of all their adventures on Vulcan.

CPSIA information can be obtained
at www.ICGtesting.com
Printed in the USA
LVHW021804080622
720759LV00003B/363